Speaking from the Heart

Speaking from the Heart

Ed Weyhing

Fathom Publishing Company

This book is a work of fiction. The characters, incidents, and dialogues are products of the author's imagination and are not to be construed as real. Any resemblance to actual events or persons, living or dead, is entirely co-incidental. References to real people, events, establishments, organizations, or locales are intended only to provide a sense of authenticity and are used fictionally.

ISBN   978-1-888215-24-3

Library of Congress Control Number: 2013947696

Cover design by Jeffrey Duckworth (duckofalltrades.com).

An earlier version of Section 1 ("Orphaned") originally appeared in **The Long Story 13** under the title "Speaking from the Heart."

www.edweyhing.com
Fathom Publishing Company
P.O. Box 200448
Anchorage, Alaska 99520-0448
Telephone /Fax907-272-3305
Printed in the United States of America

For Stephen, Paul, and Philip

For Mary

Book I

Douglastown

Section 1 — Orphaned

Nona's daughter was 14 when she became pregnant, 15 when she gave birth to the baby boy she would not live to know.

After a difficult delivery, the young mother started to bleed. By the time the midwife decided to call an ambulance, it was already too late. At that it was another 90 minutes for the ambulance to get there from Brightwood Crossing. The young mother was pronounced dead by the attendant, while the driver busied himself getting someone to sign the call slip.

Nona noticed that the baby's feet did not look right, but in the hopeless rush to save the young mother, she wrapped the infant in a blanket and laid him aside. Later, when Nona and her friend Glynnis next door tended to the baby and washed him up, they discovered what did not look right: the baby's feet were turned in and his ankles bent.

The next day Nona's neighbors and some friends of the young mother buried her body with a simple funeral from the church. Nona, distraught, stayed home with Glynis and cared for the baby. Others offered to be with the baby and let Nona attend the funeral, but Nona would not let the infant out of her grasp.

And over and over Nona would ask herself the question that would come to haunt her: *How?* How did her daughter turn from the sparkling, laughing, light-hearted young girl, bright and studious in school, her mother and father's pride and joy — how did she turn from this into the sullen teenager whose only interest was getting out of the house and hanging out with the wrong crowd?

Was it after the young girl's father, a supervisor at the quarry, was killed when a carload of rock got away and crushed him? Was it the trauma of Nona's grief over losing her husband? Was it when Nona was forced to leave her home in company housing and take her daughter to live in the Mockingbird Project in Douglastown in the Maryville Region?

What else should she have done? What *could* she have done?

As for the baby's father: it was a secret her daughter did not reveal. Certainly no one stepped forward to claim responsibility.

After the young girl was buried, her older cousin down the street and that cousin's boyfriend and his friends and some of the younger neighbors came back to the house, passed around the flasks, ate what food Nona had in the house, and bemoaned what they could not change. And of course the more they drank of the flasks, the more they cried and carried on over the death of the baby's mother, Nona's only daughter, at the age of 15.

Now you cry! Nona thought.

And after the crying and carrying on died down, and the flasks were empty, and the mother's cousin and her boyfriend and his friends and the younger neighbors had gone home, Nona and her friend Glynnis next door were able to get back to the subject of the baby and the baby's feet.

By then it was apparent that it wasn't just "something wrong." A gross deformity left the baby's feet turned in and his ankles bent, a deformity that would become more and more evident as the baby started to grow into the toddler he would become. Especially when the little boy started to take his first steps, wobbling from one side to the other, it was clear he was a severely crippled child.

Glynnis next door pronounced that a misfortune such as this was caused only by the Great Spirit. In this case, she decided, it was to avenge the evil done by his father — whoever he was and whatever terrible sin he had done, on top of the sin of abandoning such a young mother. And Glynnis, seeing the baby's feet turned in and his ankles bent, advised Nona to cover the baby's feet and ankles with blankets and not let the word get around about the great misfortune because hadn't there been enough already? With her daughter, dead at age 15? And getting over that? And why not let well enough alone?

And so Nona kept the baby wrapped in a blanket, which didn't look that unusual, a baby that little. And a good-looking baby at that. And she named the baby Mbasa Kilu, which meant "wild goat." And when her friend Glynnis next door asked why she named the baby Mbasa Kilu, which meant "wild goat," Nona said: "Because that was my father's name."

"Em-bah-sa," said Glynnis, testing the syllables on her tongue.

"Yes," said Nona. "Mbasa Kilu: that is his name."

* * * * *

Despite her grief over her daughter — in fact, all the more so *because* of it — Nona resolved that she would bring up this baby, that she would give him what she had not been able to give her daughter.

"I lost my daughter," said Nona, "but I will not lose this child." And in the years that followed Mbasa Kilu in turn loved Grandmother Nona; loved her, in fact, like he would have loved his own mother, barely a teenager, now gone to her grave.

So Mbasa Kilu spent a good deal of the early months pretty much wrapped in a blanket. And when people asked Nona about her grandson, she always said, "He'll be fine."

But her friend Glynnis next door made the gesture of *Not-Right-in-the-Head*, which people understood. Because Glynnis considered *Not-Right-in-the-Head* a lesser misfortune, like something inconvenient for now, but might be okay, say, in a year or so, or in a few months even. And Glynnis thought it best not to let word get around about the great misfortune of the feet and ankles, which was a much worse misfortune than *Not-Right-in-the-Head*, and if you saw it you knew it would *not* be okay in a few months or in a year or so or ever. Especially, reasoned Glynnis, since it was caused by the Great Spirit to avenge the sin of an evil father, whoever he was and whatever terrible deed he had done, who would then abandon such a young mother, without owning up to his responsibility for the baby he had fathered. So why not let well enough alone? Even though, of course, word *did* get around. But at least people talked about it in whispers and not directly to Nona. Which after all, after what happened to her daughter, hadn't she suffered enough?

Of course Mbasa Kilu slept very often when he was a baby. But before long he was not a baby, but a toddler. Then not a toddler, but a little boy. And a little boy couldn't sit around all day with his feet under a blanket. He wanted to be up and doing something, even if that made his wobbling steps all the more pitiful. So Nona let him play outside. "But stay in the back yard," she told him, and gave him her husband's old football out of the trunk. "This was your grandfather's," she told him, and showed him how to kick it up and down the back yard. Even with the great misfortune of the feet and ankles, Mbasa Kilu was able to kick the football up and down the back yard, which he did sometimes for hours.

Until the day he kicked the ball out of the back yard, over the fence — three times! The third time Grandmother Nona had to fetch the ball, she brought him into the lane out front, and showed him how to kick the ball into the tree. "You can do it while the kids are in school," she told him. Because in the afternoon when the kids came home from school it was time for *Every Woman's Love* and *True Crime Scenes* on TV, anyway. And every morning Mbasa Kilu enjoyed going out front in the lane and kicking the ball up into the tree and watching it bounce back down, one branch at a time.

After a few weeks of kicking the ball up into the tree and watching it bounce back down, one branch at a time, Mbasa Kilu learned to kick it higher and higher. But since he kicked by himself, nobody really noticed how high he was kicking it. When Grandmother Nona called him in for lunch and he begged for one last kick and she said okay and he kicked it, it would take longer and longer for the ball to bounce back down, one branch at a time. But Grandmother Nona thought this was just another way for him to fool around outside and not come in sooner. She didn't realize he was kicking it higher and higher. And if any of the neighbor ladies happened to look out and see him kicking in the lane, taking his wobbly steps to retrieve the ball, they said, "There's Nona's grandson again. Poor kid." Or, "He should be in school, except . . ."

And they would trail off. Or they would make the gesture of *Not-Right-in-the-Head.*

* * * * *

Now Mbasa Kilu, playing by himself, did not talk much. So Grandmother Nona did the talking for him. "You want a banana, don't you," she would say to him when he appeared by her side in the kitchen. And if Grandmother Nona did not understand, he would point to what he wanted, or reach for it. "Oh, it's a cracker you want," she would say. And — providing it was not to be had for supper — she would give it to him.

And she took him by the hand when she visited her friends for tea. "He wants a cracker," she would say to her friends. Or if there were bananas on the counter, "He sees those bananas," she would say. And her friends understood, and were glad to find something to do for the little boy who had suffered a great misfortune at birth. They could always give him a cracker, or a banana.

And that was not like saying everything was okay. Not like saying the terrible sin of his father was okay. It was like saying, *We know about the great misfortune, the feet turned in and the ankles bent.* It was like saying, *We know why it is. But still he likes to eat.*

So of course people saw the child Mbasa Kilu, and the feet turned in and the ankles bent, the way he walked with wobbly steps, and that he did not talk much, but only watched TV or kicked the football in the lane. Or that instead of asking for food, he looked at food he wanted, or reached for it without talking, or — more often than not — that Grandmother Nona anticipated it. And they accepted it, because they knew it was the result of the terrible misfortune, caused by the Great Spirit to avenge the sin of his father. But they also explained it by the gesture of *Not-Right-in-the-Head,* which was easier for people to understand, since they didn't even know who the father was, much less what evil thing he had done. So they accepted it, and they knew that once kids came home from school the boy was better safe in the house with Grandmother Nona watching *Every Woman's Love* than out in the neighborhood where some kid playing football would *Boom!* knock into him and bowl him over, and so on. And that is the story of Mbasa Kilu's childhood: *In the morning: playing in the lane with the football; and in the afternoon: safe in the house with Grandmother Nona.*

This, of course, was before the arrival of the White Franciscan Sisters, which happened the year Mbasa Kilu turned 12.

* * * * *

The year Mbasa Kilu turned 12, the White Franciscan Sisters came to Douglastown and started the Douglastown Free Lunch Program, and the Douglastown Free Breakfast Program, and the Douglastown Senior Citizens Soup Kitchen Program, and the Douglastown Home Visitation Program, and so on and so on. The White Franciscan Sisters were known as a force to be reckoned with.

When Grandmother Nona let the two sisters from the Home Visitation Team in, Mbasa Kilu was sitting in front of the TV. "He doesn't talk much," she told them. "You can ask me if you don't understand." And with that Mbasa Kilu looked up and said, *"Channel 11 — the Station that Greets the Nation!"* And: *"Even upside down, it's still an X!"* And then he pointed at the kitchen counter. *"He wants one of those bananas he sees on the counter!"* he said. So much for the boy who did not talk much.

After that, when the sisters talked to Grandmother Nona, they did not buy the gesture of *Not-Right-in-the-Head*, and did not buy the idea of safe in the house watching *Every Woman's Love,* and did not buy the fear of out in the neighborhood *Boom!* Mbasa Kilu getting bowled over, and so on.

So they came in the White Van and hauled Mbasa Kilu and Grandmother Nona off to see the principal at the White Franciscan Sisters' School and had the White Franciscan Sisters' School Psychologist test Mbasa Kilu. "He won't answer you," said Grandmother Nona. But after receiving an M&M candy for his first answer, Mbasa Kilu spoke up and answered all the test questions of the White Franciscan Sisters School Psychologist. And she found that watching *Every Woman's Love* (and — when Grandmother Nona dozed off in her chair — *Sesame Street* and CNN *World News Tonight*) and reading TV Guide and the directions on instant soup and so on, placed Mbasa Kilu, age 12, on a second-grade level in language and reading skills. And probably beyond that in number skills because he knew "one and one-half cups of water" and "boil for 30 seconds" and "3:30pm on Channel 11" and so on, even though he didn't understand plus, minus, multiply, and divide.

So much for the gesture of *Not-Right-in-the-Head*. So much for the fear of *Boom!* bowled over, and so on. The White Franciscan Sisters told Grandmother Nona the White Van would be there every morning at 7:30 to pick up Mbasa Kilu and deliver him to the White Franciscan Sisters' School, where during the first summer he spent every morning in the computer learning center and soon understood plus, minus, multiply, and divide, and by September, age 13, was ready to enter fourth grade, only four years behind. Furthermore, after six years' watching *Every Woman's Love,* there were plenty of ways he was four years *ahead!*

From then on Grandmother Nona did not use the gesture of *Not-Right-in-the-Head*, which she had started to feel uncomfortable with anyway, seeing how bright he was growing up to be. And as for the revenge of the Great Spirit, sometimes Grandmother Nona thought, How can the Great Spirit wish to take revenge on a newborn baby? Why would a spirit who is great do such a thing? She did not know the answer, but she no longer accepted the idea of revenge. Especially the idea of punishing the father for his sin by wreaking revenge on this innocent baby, her grandson.

* * * * *

It was here, at the White Franciscan Sisters' School, Mbasa Kilu first learned about the job of Mission Caretaker, because the principal of the White Franciscan Sisters' School said Mbasa Kilu should learn job skills, which he did by staying after school and sweeping up the classrooms after class and helping Mister Winston, who was a great-grandfather from the U.S.A., wash windows and clean up the Boys' Room. And the principal of the White Franciscan Sisters' School gave Mbasa Kilu a check every two weeks for this staying and sweeping and so on, and, of course, Grandmother Nona was glad to see the check, even though the neighbor lady, who watched CNN and *Courtroom of the Air* and was wise in such matters, said: "I mean, *fourth grade!* Aren't there child labor laws?" But of course, Mbasa Kilu was 13, even though only in fourth grade, and Grandmother Nona made the *What-Can-I-Say?* gesture, because she liked the extra check every two weeks, which bought milk and bread but also four or five extra lottery tickets, and anyway: Who would be crazy enough to tangle with the White Franciscan Sisters?

So the White Franciscan Sisters taught Mbasa Kilu academics, and they saw that he learned job skills from Mister Winston the Mission Caretaker, who was a great-grandfather. But they also tried to help him, though to no avail, with the problem of the feet turned in and the ankles bent. The White Franciscan Nurse Sister at the White Franciscan Sisters' School made arrangements for Grandmother Nona to take Mbasa Kilu to various doctors in nearby villages, paying their cab fare both ways. And once the White Franciscan Nurse Sister drove Mbasa Kilu and Grandmother Nona all the way to the Imperial Medical Center Annex in Brightwood Crossing to see the Big Doctor there. But every place it was the same story: every doctor said, "If we had seen him before he was a year old. . . . Even before he was a month old. . ."

And this, of course, depressed Grandmother Nona, because she knew the doctors and the Big Doctor at the Imperial Medical Center Annex in Brightwood Crossing could have helped Mbasa Kilu. Even though her friend Glynnis next door said the doctors did not understand the workings of the Great Spirit. Because, she said, it was the Great Spirit who laid this affliction on Mbasa Kilu, avenging the sin of his father. She also said that whether Mbasa Kilu was a month old, or a year old, or 5 years old, or 13 years old, which he then was, there was no getting around the Great Spirit. But Grandmother Nona no longer believed this, no longer believed that the Great Spirit had revenge on her grandson, and so she stopped talking about it with her friend Glynnis.

* * * * *

Then there was the girl Ofi Leiya. At the White Franciscan Sisters' School Mbasa Kilu had trouble with spelling words. And the girl Ofi Leiya, who was 9, and known by the White Franciscan Sisters to be at the top of the class in every subject, including spelling words, was assigned by the White Franciscan Fourth Grade Teacher Sister to hear Mbasa Kilu's spelling words and to teach him the spelling of words he did not know. And, in fact, it was Ofi Leiya, then only 9, who discovered that Mbasa Kilu wasn't really hearing the sounds of words the same as everybody else, and the White Franciscan Sisters' School Nurse checked Mbasa Kilu's hearing and ears and discovered he had a chronic ear infection which stopped up his ears and made sounds seem different to him. And Grandmother Nona was given four weeks of antibiotic pills to give Mbasa Kilu. And soon his ear infection was cured, once and for all, and he heard the same sounds as everyone else.

So Mbasa Kilu learned spelling words, and got rid of his ear infection, and from then on he did better in school, and heard Grandmother Nona more clearly, and heard better the sounds of *Every Woman's Love* and CNN *World News Tonight* and even the whispers of those who made the gestures of *Not-Right-in-the-Head* when he passed. So the girl Ofi Leiya, though she was only 9, and four years younger than Mbasa Kilu, helped him with spelling words, and the ear infection, and so on. And played a key role in getting him off to a good start at the White Franciscan Sisters' School.

And that is the story of how Ofi Leiya met Mbasa Kilu, and what part she played in his early life.

* * * * *

So Mbasa Kilu was doing better with his spelling words, and hearing better, and doing well in school, overall, considering he was four years behind his age group. But he was not doing well in all ways, and often he thought of the days of sitting safe at home beside Grandmother Nona watching *Every Woman's Love*. And this is the story of some of the ways Mbasa Kilu was *not* doing well.

First, there was the classroom. Kids remembered all those years of the *Not-Right-in-the-Head* gesture. So when he missed a spelling word or got a multiply or divide wrong, somebody would make the gesture of *Not-Right-in-the-Head*. Especially since he was taller than every other kid, why shouldn't he know even harder spelling words and tougher multiply and divides? *Not-Right-in-the-Head*, kids said. *That's why.*

The girl Ofi Leiya, 9 years old and thought to be tops in every subject, held her breath when it was Mbasa Kilu's turn at spelling words. She did not pay attention to *Not-Right-in-the-Head*. Nor did the White Franciscan Sisters, nor Mister Winston, the great-grandfather from the U.S.A., who taught Mbasa Kilu the job of Mission Caretaker, and saw how clever he was, despite the feet turned in and the ankles bent.

Okay, but this is not the story of clever. It is the story of not-so-good. And in spite of clever, there were plenty of ways in which Mbasa Kilu was doing not-so-good. For example, the playground, the second example of not-so-good. Even with his feet turned in and his ankles bent, Mbasa Kilu was taller than all the kids by several inches. But he was never chosen for football by the kids in his class. Why? Because try throwing him the ball. *Boom!* Off his chest. Try kicking him the ball. *Boom!* Between his legs, or off his nose. All those early years of *Every Woman's Love* and "boil for thirty seconds" plus the feet turned in and the ankles bent didn't make Mbasa Kilu better on the playground. CNN *World News* couldn't prevent *Boom!* off his chest. Even kicking the ball in the lane all morning couldn't prevent *Boom!* off his chest. Thus Mbasa Kilu was never chosen for football by the kids in his class. Sister Ann McDermott — in charge of playground — saw this. So she took aside Tedu Ngraeba. "Why can't Mbasa Kilu be allowed to play?" she asked. "Why can't one of the teams choose him?"

Now Tedu Ngraeba was the tallest boy in school. He carried the gold cross at the head of processions. He was thought to be the undisputed number one on the football pitch. But he was also a leader, and that is why Sister Ann McDermott took him aside.

He explained the situation to Sister Ann McDermott. He would not allow other kids to snicker at Mbasa Kilu, or make gestures of *Not-Right-in-the-Head*. But, of course, he did not choose him for football, either. Who would? What with *Boom!* off his chest? Instead, he proposed a compromise to Sister Ann McDermott. Tedu Ngraeba said he would teach Mbasa Kilu to kick the ball — but on the sideline, where there was no danger of *Boom!* off his chest. That way the game would not have to be slowed down for the other boys, but Mbasa Kilu could still play. On the sideline, of course.

The White Franciscan Sisters were not big on compromises, but because it was Tedu Ngraeba, Sister Ann McDermott agreed to give it a try. That afternoon Tedu Ngraeba took Mbasa Kilu aside to teach him to kick the ball into the practice goal, which was off to the side. On the very first attempt Mbasa Kilu demonstrated the style he had learned in the lane, which was to kick the ball high in the air — far higher than any goal. After the fourth such attempt it was clear Mbasa Kilu had his own unique style of kicking. So Tedu Ngraeba gave an extra football to Mbasa Kilu on the sidelines. *Practice kicking at the Great Oak Tree,* he told Mbasa Kilu. And Tedu Ngraeba made a fist at any boy who snickered. So that was how Tedu Ngraeba was involved.

* * * * *

And so, finally, the third part of the story of not-so-good. Even if Mbasa Kilu got all his spelling words right, even if on the sidelines he managed to kick the extra football *Smack!* into the great oak tree, there was the great affliction of his birth, the misfortune laid on him by whoever caused it, for whatever reason. Doing better with his spelling words and plus and minus and so on did not change the fact that Mbasa Kilu had the great affliction of his feet turned in and his ankles bent. And this misfortune he had to deal with every morning from the moment he set foot out the front door to walk down the sidewalk to the White Van. And if you don't know what it felt like and looked like, just try walking out your front door and down your front sidewalk to the White Van, wobbling from side to side, and up the front sidewalk of school with all the kids standing around before the bell rings, and down the hall to the classroom and down to the lunchroom and back up to the Computer Learning Center, and so on and so on, with your feet turned in and your ankles bent. Try doing that every morning. *Not-so-good,* you would say. *Not-so-good!*

* * * * *

And one other thing happened one morning at the White Franciscan Sisters' School. One other thing neither good nor bad, but which got attention. Some boys were playing with the football in front of school, before the bell rang, and the ball got away. Walking up the front walk of school, his feet turned in and his ankles bent, Mbasa Kilu saw the ball rolling toward him — and he kicked it, just like he kicked his grandfather's football at home in the lane. And the ball soared up over the school entrance, onto the roof. Mr. Winston, the Mission Caretaker, had to be called to unlock the third floor storage and open the attic window so one of the boys could climb out and get it. And from then on Mbasa Kilu was known not only as the boy with the feet turned in and the ankles bent, but the boy who kicked the ball on the roof.

* * * * *

Next was Maryville Regional Vocational High School, where Mbasa Kilu and his classmates went after they graduated from the White Franciscan Sisters' School. The Maryville

Regional Vocational High School was on the grounds of the old Imperial College, which of course was abandoned during the war and never started up again. And the Maryville Regional Vocational High School was actually run by the Brothers of St. Columban, who could have called it St. Columban Vocational High School or St. Peter Claver or St. Somebody but called it Maryville Regional Vocational High School in order to get Revenue Sharing Grants from the Imperial Government, which was a joke, since the Imperial Government went broke. At least, after the government officials were paid off and the police and the military officers were paid off there was nothing left for vocational high schools and Revenue Sharing Grants and so on. But at one time there was hope of grants for training boys to learn a trade like carpenter and stonemason and machine repair and the girls to weave brightly colored cloth and be nurses and later midwives and so on.

And for Mbasa Kilu it was still no picnic, but at least better. By the time he went to Maryville Regional Vocational High School, Mbasa Kilu took the regular school bus, even though he still wobbled from side to side when he walked, with his ankles bent and his feet turned in. And riding the regular school bus made him feel more like his classmates, listening to their jokes and shouts, being pushed and jostled around getting off the bus, going up the front walk of the school in a crowd. At least there wasn't any White Van, no going up the front walk by himself, with everyone staring, and so on.

And there was football. At Maryville Regional Vocational High School football was Number One. And Number One in football was Tedu Ngraeba, who in grade school was the tallest boy, in grade school carried the cross at the head of processions, and now was the tallest and fastest boy at Maryville Regional Vocational High School, and captain of the football team. Tedu Ngraeba scored more goals, made more blocks, played more minutes, headed off more passes, committed fewer fouls than any player ever to attend Maryville Regional Vocational High School. Tedu Ngraeba was the best football player ever to come from the Maryville Region, the best ever in the entire Rangala Province. Long before he graduated from the Maryville Regional Vocational High School Tedu Ngraeba was a sure bet for the Douglastown Leopards.

And Tedu Ngraeba still looked out for Mbasa Kilu. Every player knew Tedu Ngraeba wouldn't stand still for any of the gestures of *Not-Right-in-the-Head*. And Tedu Ngraeba appointed Mbasa Kilu Official Mascot of the Maryville Regional Vocational High School team, and always greeted him with *Nwoso!*, which means fearsome, which was a battle cry of the Maryville Regional Vocational High School team, which the team shouted in unison when they broke their huddle. And when the team broke their huddle, and in unison shouted *Nwoso!*, Tedu Ngraeba would point *Good Health!* to Mbasa Kilu, and Mbasa Kilu would smile and point *Good Health!* back. And then Tedu Ngraeba would trot out to his position in the field.

During the team's practice Tedu Ngraeba made sure Mbasa Kilu had an extra football on the sidelines to kick at the great oak tree, since he was the mascot of the team, even though he could never play a regular game, because of his feet turned in and his ankles bent.

And Ofi Leiya too was there at the Maryville Regional Vocational High School. And in the halls she smiled at Mbasa Kilu and said his name, and did not look down at his feet like many did, and did not pretend not to see him, like others did. And Ofi Leiya now and then put her tray beside his in the cafeteria, when she was not surrounded by her friends and admirers, and asked him about his Shop Project, and Business I; and Ofi Leiya encouraged him about Speech I, which he hated, and gave him ideas of what to talk about, and what to say, and how to look them in the eye and say what he felt, from his heart. Which, of course, Mbasa Kilu could never do when he stood in front of Speech I. But he liked to hear Ofi Leiya talk about his heart, and he thought about it for days after. And he even managed to get through his speech class final exam, which was a how-to speech. In his speech, he explained how to program the VCR to tape *Every Woman's Love* when you were at school, which none of the others in the class understood, and even Sister Melissa Perkins, the Speech Teacher, did not understand, but Mbasa Kilu got C-plus for the speech anyway, which was a good grade.

* * * * * .

Another time in Speech I, the boys and girls were told to give a talk to the class about what they liked about their mother and father. And Sister Melissa Perkins realized the minute she gave the assignment that at least six students had no father and were being raised by a single mother, and Mbasa Kilu had neither a mother nor a father, but was being raised by his grandmother. So she added that students could talk about their mother or father or both, or grandmother or grandfather or anyone who helped raise them. Mbasa Kilu knew it would be easy to say things about Grandmother Nona. But it caused him to think, *Who are my mother and father?*

Mbasa Kilu realized that anytime he brought this up to Grandmother Nona she would put him off, or tell him "later." But this time he told his Grandmother Nona that he *really* needed to know. "For class," he told her. And he told her about Sister Melissa Perkins' assignment, without mentioning that a grandmother or a grandfather or whoever takes care of you was okay.

So Grandmother Nona, seeing that he was determined to find out, told him what she thought was best for him to hear, that his mother and father had become seriously ill and died just after he was born. But that she, Grandmother Nona, loved him and would always be there to take care of him.

Mbasa Kilu listened, and hugged her when she started to cry at the end. But at least he now had the story.

And in class he talked about his Grandmother Nona. He said that she cooked good meals and gave him clean clothes to wear to school. He said that she watched *Every Woman's Love* with him, even though she wasn't interested in CNN *World News Tonight*. He said that she loved him and would always be there to take care of him.

"Mbasa Kilu, that was wonderful," whispered Ofi Leiya when he returned to his seat.

At home that night, Mbasa Kilu decided to do what they had been taught in *Writing*.

He opened his writing notebook to a new page, and at the top he printed *Journal*. And next he wrote: *"My name is Mbasa Kilu. I was born to parents who would have become rich had they not become sick and died shortly after I was born. My Grandmother Nona loves me and will always be there to take care of me."*

* * * * * .

And Mbasa Kilu went to every football practice, and on the sidelines kicked the extra football at the great oak tree.

And Mbasa Kilu, even though he could never play a regular game, could never play on the regular field, because of his feet turned in and his ankles bent, became good on the sidelines, and learned to kick the extra football at the great oak tree, high into the branches of the great oak tree, and learned to kick the extra football on a straight line at the great oak tree, even from thirty meters away, even from forty.

And Mbasa Kilu liked kicking the extra football, and liked the feel of the ball off his left foot turned in, liked seeing the ball soar into the upper branches of the great oak tree. And he liked the idea that members of the team noticed him kicking the extra football, and sometimes encouraged him. "Give it a ride, Mbasa Kilu!" they would say. Sometimes during a break in practice they would encourage him. "Give it a ride, Mbasa Kilu! See how high you can put it." "Let's see you hit the tree, Mbasa Kilu," they would say. And Mbasa Kilu would kick the ball high into the great oak tree. And the team would cheer as the ball bounced off the branches on its long way back down.

Once when the ball bounced back to the ground, it hit the red garbage can at the corner of the pitch, dislodging the lid with a loud clang. This gave rise to a new trick, a new recreation for the team before and after practice and at time outs in their drills. "Let's see you hit the can, Mbasa Kilu," they would say. So Mbasa Kilu in his spare time practiced a different kick, a looping kick into the corner which always landed within a meter or two of the can, and one out of three times hit it.

Yet, for Mbasa Kilu, in the final analysis, it came down to this: How many goals are you awarded for kicking the ball high into the great oak tree? Answer: none. How many goals are you awarded for hitting the red can? Answer: none. And what position can you play with your feet turned in and your ankles bent? Answer: none.

Yet even though he could never play a regular game, because of his feet turned in and his ankles bent, Mbasa Kilu dreamed of taking the field with Tedu Ngraeba, dreamed of playing beside Tedu Ngraeba, playing in the championship game, and he dreamed of Tedu Ngraeba double-teamed, and Tedu Ngraeba unable to take a shot on goal, and Tedu Ngraeba passing the ball to him, Mbasa Kilu. And Mbasa Kilu dreamed of taking the pass on the left sideline with six seconds to play and the score tied, and dreamed of advancing toward the goal and kicking the ball past the Harbourtown keeper. *Nwoso!* The winning goal!

And Mbasa Kilu dreamed these things on the sidelines, kicking the extra ball, and dreamed at night as well. And sometimes in his dreams, the crowds shouted and streamed onto the field and lifted him up, and reporters crowded around and asked him how he felt, and Ofi Leiya herself was the KXR13-TV announcer, and put a microphone in front of him and said, *How do you feel, Mbasa Kilu? How do you feel?*

And in composition class, thinking of what to write about, Mbasa Kilu sometimes thought of writing these things, about taking the pass from Tedu Ngraeba, about kicking the winning goal past the Harbourtown Voc-Tech keeper. But he didn't know how to start, so instead he took the suggestion of Sister Melissa Perkins and wrote about the great oak tree and the leaves and how the leaves changed their colors and how they fell to the ground before winter. But still he dreamed of the winning goal, and dreamed of writing about it some day. Dreamed of writing his own memoirs in a book which would be placed on the shelf at the White Franciscan Sisters' School, alongside the biography of President Robert Kloboso and the memoirs of Brigadier General Solomon Gambwizi, both now dead, and *Profiles in Courage,* by President John F. Kennedy of the U.S.A., also now dead.

Some day, perhaps. But until that day, Mbasa Kilu remained the mascot of the Maryville Regional Vocational High School team, and shouted *Nwoso!* when the team broke their huddle and headed onto the field, and pointed *Good Health!* to Tedu Ngraeba when he scored a goal or stole a pass or blocked a shot.

* * * * *

And so for Mbasa Kilu the Maryville Regional Vocational High School, run by the Brothers of St. Columban, though it was no particular picnic, was at least better. And he learned carpenter and stonemason and machinery repair, and he walked up the steps of the regular school bus himself, and was pushed and jostled along with the other students, and listened to their laughing and their jokes, and walked up the front walk in a crowd of students instead of by himself, and was Official Mascot of the Maryville Regional Vocational High School team.

And Mbasa Kilu and his class went from Freshman to Sophomore to Junior and finally to Senior which meant Graduation and Getting Jobs, which was on the minds of all the members of his class. And also on the minds of some of the better football players was promotion from the Maryville Regional High School team to the Douglastown Leopards professional team.

And one day in shop class, Brother Mortimer Ygloso, the shop teacher, himself a graduate of the Maryville Regional Vocational High School, announced a job opening, as he did from time to time. This opening was for the job of Mission Caretaker. Mister Winston, the great-grandfather from the U.S.A., was for years the Mission Caretaker, since before the White Franciscan Sisters' House was built, back when the Church of St. Peter Claver was the only Mission Building. Mister Winston was to return to the U.S.A., and Brother Mortimer Ygloso, the shop teacher at the Maryville Regional Vocational High School, himself a former student and graduate of that school, announced that the job of Mission Caretaker would be open.

Most of the boys in the shop class wanted to be carpenters or mechanics with public works or one of the contractors and paid little attention to the announcement about Mission Caretaker. Mbasa Kilu, however, was interested in Mister Winston's job, in the job of Mission Caretaker, because Mbasa Kilu had already worked for Mister Winston for several years, and was familiar with his job, and knew that part of Mister Winston's job, part of the job of Mission Caretaker, was to drive the Great Gasoline-Powered Lawn Mower over the grounds of the Mission Compound, over the lawns and around the trees and around the edge of the flower gardens, even onto the terraces sloping down to the edge of the precipice overlooking the Great River, which roared through the gorge, eating everything in its path.

And Mbasa Kilu got the application form from the Mission Secretary and filled it in, listing his date of birth and history of classes at the Maryville Regional Vocational High School, and his grades. And at the end of the form it said *Do you have any disability preventing you from performing the duties of _____?* And Mbasa Kilu thought of his feet turned in and his ankles bent, and he thought about the Great Misfortune of his birth, and he even thought of the gestures of *Not-Right-in-the-Head.*

But then he realized the Mission Secretary had forgotten to fill in the blank, so that the form said *the duties of (blank),* and for all intents and purposes the question read *Do you have any disability preventing you from performing the duties of Nothing?* which surely must be no duties at all. And Mbasa Kilu thought about this for a while. And he thought that no disability would prevent him from performing no duties at all, not even the Great Misfortune of the feet turned in and the ankles bent, not even if it was caused by the Revenge of the Great Spirit for the sin of his father, even though his Grandmother Nona no longer believed this, and so on. And for a minute Mbasa Kilu thought of this as the correct answer on the application form. But he didn't feel easy about this, because he realized the Mission Secretary had forgotten to fill in the blank, and he realized he was hiding behind the Mission Secretary's forgetting. And he thought of the White Franciscan Sisters finding him in the Home Visitation Program, and taking him and Grandmother Nona in the White Van to see the principal of the White Franciscan Sisters' School, and not being satisfied with safe at home watching *Every Woman's Love.* And he thought of how many times he walked up the front sidewalk at the White Franciscan Sisters' School with his feet turned in and his ankles bent, and with all the kids standing around before the bell rang. And Mbasa Kilu thought about Ofi Leiya and the spelling words, and he thought about the Computer Learning Center, and the gestures of *Not-Right-in-the-Head.* And he thought about the speech before Sister Melissa Perkins's speech class, about how to program the VCR to record *Every Woman's Love* even when you would not be home to watch it.

And Mbasa Kilu did not like the idea of hiding behind what the Mission Secretary forgot to fill in, and he took his pencil, and filled in himself what the Mission Secretary forgot, so the question read *Do you have any disability preventing you from performing the duties of Mission Caretaker?* And when he had filled in the question with the words "Mission Caretaker," he thought of himself, Mbasa Kilu, with his feet turned in and his ankles bent, starting up the Great Gasoline-Powered Lawn Mower, steering it over the lawns of the Mission Compound, over the terraces and hills, around the flower beds and trees,

even onto the terraces sloping down to the precipice overlooking the Great River, which roared through the gorge
eating everything in its path. And when he saw in his mind
the picture of himself riding the Great Gasoline-Powered Lawn
Mower, performing the duties of Mission Caretaker, he knew
he could do it. And he took his pencil and wrote the answer
to the question. *No,* he wrote. *No.* He had no disability preventing him from performing the duties of Mission Caretaker.
And when he filled in No, he folded the application and gave
it back to the Mission Secretary, stuck the Mission Secretary's
pencil in his pocket, and headed for football practice.

* * * * *

When Tedu Ngraeba arrived at practice that day, Mbasa
Kilu was already there, on the sidelines, with the extra football,
kicking it high into the great oak tree. Tedu Ngraeba, when he
saw Mbasa Kilu practicing, called out and waved. And he could
tell that Mbasa Kilu was serious about kicking the football
into the great oak tree this day, though he did not know that
Mbasa Kilu, while he kicked the ball, thought of the job of
Mission Caretaker, and thought of the Great Gasoline-Powered Lawn Mower, and pictured himself riding the Great Gasoline-Powered Lawn Mower around the lawns of the Mission
Compound, around the borders of flower beds, over hills and
terraces, even onto the terraces sloping down to the precipice
overlooking the Great River, which thundered through the
gorge below, eating everything in its path.

And when the next players drifted in and Tedu Ngraeba
heard them call out to Mbasa Kilu and tease him about his
kicking into the great oak tree, and tease him about being
serious, Tedu Ngraeba signaled them to shut up and knock
off the teasing and put their cleats on. And when one of the
players made the mistake of making the gesture of *Not-Right-
in-the-Head* Tedu Ngraeba put a stop to it.

And not only would Tedu Ngraeba not stand still for the
gestures of *Not-Right-in-the-Head,* but when there was a timeout
in the practice he made the Maryville Regional players stop and
watch Mbasa Kilu, and made them clap and shout encouragement to him on the sidelines with the extra ball as he kicked
it — *Boom!* — high into the great oak tree thirty meters, even
forty meters away.

Now Mbasa Kilu liked Tedu Ngraeba for this, and liked the cheers and encouragement as he kicked the extra ball into the great oak tree. But he knew that the extra ball was not the same as playing on the football team for the Maryville Regional Vocational High School. And when Tedu Ngraeba was not there to give him the extra ball, he often wouldn't get it, and when Tedu Ngraeba was not there to stop them, sometimes there was the intentional mistake of *Owasi Kilu,* which means "wounded goat," instead of Mbasa Kilu, his name.

And the same day that he had submitted his application for Mission Caretaker, during another timeout at practice, after Mbasa Kilu had kicked the extra ball high into the great oak tree, forty meters away, one of the players, in fact the same player who had made the gesture of *Not-Right-in-the-Head*, said, "Why doesn't Mbasa Kilu try kicking it into the regular goal?" And then there was an argument about the feet turned in and the ankles bent, and about the Great Spirit, and about Mbasa Kilu's mother, and the sin of his father, and the Great Misfortune, and why Mbasa Kilu couldn't play on the regular pitch, and why he couldn't kick at the regular goal, and even some gestures of *Not-Right-in-the-Head*, until Tedu Ngraeba put a stop to that. And finally somebody just rolled the ball out to midfield, and said just try. And others said, "Go ahead, Mbasa Kilu." And others said "Give it a ride!" And so on. And Tedu Ngraeba, seeing it would be as much embarrassment to Mbasa Kilu if he wasn't allowed to try, as it would be if he tried and failed, nodded to him and said, "Go ahead, Mbasa Kilu. Give it a ride!"

And Mbasa Kilu, who had never kicked the ball on the actual football pitch before, and had never even *been* on the pitch except to draw the lines or mow the grass or pick up after practice, walked out to midfield. And all the players were watching, and a few of their girlfriends who came along and were watching practice, and some of the old guys from the nearby village who hung around the field on practice days, and even Brother James Connelly, who taught Accounting I and II, but was the coach of Youth Football at St. Peter Claver and intensely interested in this team, most of whom had played for him. He was standing beside the pitch, watching practice and smoking a pipe. And with all these people watching, it felt to Mbasa Kilu like grade school again, getting out of the White

Van, walking up the front walk of the school. But Tedu Ngraeba nodded to him and encouraged him, and others shouted Give it a ride, Mbasa Kilu! and so on. And he finally looked at the ball, and looked at the goal forty meters away, and looked at Jeremiah Ngloso, the keeper, standing in front of the net, his hands at his side, looking like he didn't know whether he was supposed to try to block it or not. And Mbasa Kilu closed off his mind, and shut out the players on the sidelines, and shut out the shouts of the old guys from the nearby village, and even shut out the nods and encouragement of Tedu Ngraeba, and looked at the ball lying there at midfield, and looked at the goal forty meters away, and looked at Jeremiah Ngloso, the keeper, standing in front of the net, his hands at his side, not knowing whether to block it or not. And Mbasa Kilu finally pretended Jeremiah Ngloso was the great oak tree, and he looked at the ball, and kicked it straight at Jeremiah Ngloso. And straight it went. But Jeremiah Ngloso didn't even raise his arms from his side, because though the kick went straight toward the goal, it took off, and went up, and up, and passed far above the net.

And there was a noise from the players and the few girl-friends and the old guys on the sidelines, some disappointment, some surprise, some satisfaction that things had worked out right, as some said, that the Great Spirit's Will had been done. And those who had talked about the revenge of the Great Spirit now said *I told you so!* and *There! You see?* and so on. And others who thought the Great Spirit wasn't on one side or the other and had bet he could do it said *Move it closer.* But at thirty meters it was the same, the ball soaring high over the net. And some of those who had joked *Not-Right-in-the-Head* now joked that the birds better look out when Mbasa Kilu was kicking and joked that the Imperial Air Force would hire Mbasa Kilu as anti-aircraft fire and so on. And others wanted to try it closer still, and others tried to show him the proper form of kicking, and how to make the ball hit the net. But it was the same at twenty meters, and ten meters, where even Tedu Ngraeba's five-year-old nephew could kick the ball into the net. And when Mbasa Kilu changed his kicking form, as some showed him, so the ball would go lower, into the net — when he made these changes the fire went out of his kick, so the ball trickled, yes, in a straight line and toward the net, but when it got there Jeremiah Ngloso easily swept it to the side.

"But after all, what could you expect?" the naysayers said. Weren't Mbasa Kilu's feet still turned in, and his ankles still bent? And didn't everyone know of the Great Misfortune? And didn't everyone know of the Great Spirit's Will? And Vengeance? (Even though his Grandmother Nona and the White Franciscan Sisters had told him not to believe this.) And so on and on, until Tedu Ngraeba put a stop to it, and said it was time for practice to resume, and the real players took the field again, and the old guys and the few girlfriends settled into the bleachers with their Royal Crown Colas, or drifted off to the drugstore.

And Mbasa Kilu went back to the sidelines, and kicked the extra ball high into the great oak tree, not thirty, or forty, or even fifty, but sixty meters away, and knew he would never be able to hit the net, even at practice, even with nobody guarding him, and would never play beside Tedu Ngraeba, and would never be a star in the Maryville Region of the Continental Football League, and would never be interviewed by Ofi Leiya for KXR13-TV, and would never be asked by Ofi Leiya *How Do You Feel?* and would never write his memoirs, and never play the role of himself in a mini-series on TV.

* * * * *

One other person connected with this incident: Marvin Kindola. Marvin Kindola attended Maryville Regional Vocational High School. He also happened to be Tedu Ngraeba's cousin. Though their mothers were sisters, no two people were ever more unlike. For one thing, Marvin Kindola (unlike Tedu Ngraeba) did not have a father to protect him and teach him and earn money to pay for his needs. Marvin Kindola's father became interested in other women when Marvin was still an infant, spent less and less time at home, and eventually abandoned his wife and baby son, without the benefit of a divorce or a goodbye. And another thing, Marvin Kindola did not play football, or any other sport. But since they lived close together, Marvin Kindola and Tedu Ngraeba had played together as children. And Tedu Ngraeba had always been told, "Look after Marvin," and when they were young boys Tedu had appointed himself to do just that, to look after Marvin.

Marvin was in Mbasa Kilu's Business I class, and was always asking to "look at" his homework—"just to check my answers," was how he put it. And sometimes he would buy Mbasa Kilu a soda in the lunchroom, or a bag of yam crisps. He seemed to have money for such things, even though his mother was poor. Some days he came to practice and hung around with the old guys in the stands. He would quietly bet with them on this and that — which tree a bird would first alight in, whether it would rain the next day, who would make the next successful kick in practice, whether the next kick would go in the goal or miss. Quietly, they did this, and quietly exchanged money, because Brother James Connelly did not like the betting, and would put a stop to it. Except that Marvin Kindola always had an excuse: so-and-so owed me for his Royal Crown Cola and was just paying me back, and so on. And the day Mbasa Kilu failed to kick the ball into the goal, even though he could kick it far above and way beyond the goal, Marvin Kindola was in the stands, hanging with the old guys from the village. And Mbasa Kilu saw him quietly collecting money afterward, and he knew that Marvin Kindola had bet against his kick, bet that it would *not* go into the goal. In fact, he wondered if Marvin Kindola had instigated the whole affair, in order to bet on it.

And the next time that Marvin Kindola asked to "look at" Mbasa Kilu's Business I homework, he not only bought him a Royal Crown Cola in the lunchroom, but gave him a five-hundred tilota bill. Even though it was only an hour's wages by most standards, it was enough for a sandwich. So Marvin Kindola gave him enough for a sandwich. This was where Marvin Kindola fit in.

* * * * *

And by the way, the good news: there were two applicants for the job of Mission Caretaker. One was a grandfather who died of liver cancer before a decision could be reached. The other, of course, was Mbasa Kilu, who liked the idea of the Great Gasoline-Powered Lawn Mower, because he had never been permitted to drive a car, because of his Great Misfortune at birth, the unfortunate illness of his feet and ankles, which caused him to walk with his feet turned in and his ankles bent, for which he would have been denied a driver's license. And who would have allowed Mbasa Kilu to drive a car, anyway? And because Mbasa Kilu was recommended by Mister Winston — who knew what a hard worker he was and knew how clever he was — and because he was the only other applicant he was chosen for the job of Mission Caretaker.

* * * * *

In this small corner of the former Imperial College, four buildings were used by Brother Jerome Jenkins and Sister Sheila McMurphy for the Mission Center. One was the former Faculty Club of the Imperial College, which became the house of the Brothers of St. Columban, where the Mission House-keeper was in charge, and the Mission Office, where the Mission Secretary worked, typing memos and letters to the Archbishop in Indoniva, and lists of Mass and Prayer Intentions and Times, and parts of hymns that were not contained in the Mission Hymnbook. The house of the Brothers of St. Columban also contained the Mission Recreation Center, where the dances were held when the weather was chilly and when there was not a campfire to be held outside, and where the plays and choral concerts of the children were held, and where at one end stood the renamed Mission Jukebox, which was simply the jukebox from the old Student Center of the Imperial College, but which now contained only hymns and songs such as "Bright Golden Day" and *"O Salutaris"* and "The Little Drummer Boy," although Mbasa Kilu saved a couple of the small black plastic disks Brother Jerome Jenkins gave him to throw away — one called "Blue Suede Shoes," one called "Itty Bitty Peesa Weesa Action Jaction" — which Mbasa Kilu planned sometime to slip into the Mission Jukebox and play, sometime when *all* the Brothers of St. Columban *and* the Mission Housekeeper were *all* gone from the house at the same time, which in eight and one-half years never happened.

Another building was the garage containing the chickens and the store of yams and sugar beets brought by the people as offerings. A third was the shed where the Great Gasoline-Powered Lawn Mower was kept and where the generator ran when it was necessary to supply electricity for the Mission Compound, because the Imperial Government Electricity could not be relied on since the Imperial Government went broke and all the money from the Treasury was looted.

Then there was the Mission Center Annex building, formerly known as Moru Hall, the fourth and largest building remaining, which, of course, is where the ladies worked, making their brightly colored rugs, and at the rear Mbasa Kilu's apartment, which was one room and a hot plate and an electric fan and a television and a VCR, though there was no cable to hook the television to and the only tapes for the VCR were "Monsignor Fulton J. Sheen" and "The Greatest Story Ever Told," which was another problem Mbasa Kilu was working on.

Despite having to spend a lot of time working in the hot sun, Mbasa Kilu actually enjoyed the job of Mission Caretaker. Especially he liked starting the engine of the Great Gasoline-Powered Lawn Mower and steering it over the lawn of the Mission Compound, formerly the Imperial College, around the Mission Center Annex building, formerly Moru Hall.

And he felt a sense of pride about his new responsibilities. Every morning it was up to him to unlock the Mission Center Annex building and raise the huge garage doors at the end of the building and see that the huge fans were working before the ladies arrived for work. And every evening, he swept out the Mission Center Annex building of the brightly colored threads and remnants from the weaving of rugs, and carried out the candy wrappers and soft-drink cans and milk cartons left by the ladies during afternoon break, and gathered and carried out the old newspapers which on sewing days were cut up into patterns. Then, of course, he had to gather all this together with the trash from the sweeping, and the trash set out by the Mission Housekeeper, and carry it to the landfill, which was wherever it landed on the banks of the Great River which roared through the gorge, clearing everything in its path.

He also had to help with the chickens for Brother Jerome Jenkins and the garden for the Mission Housekeeper. It was his responsibility to tend to the fence around the yard where the chickens stayed, to gather eggs and give them to the Mission Housekeeper, and (whenever Brother Jerome Jenkins complained) to hose down the concrete floor of the garage where the chickens went at night.

He stored in the loft of the garage, the yams and sugar beets brought to the Mission Center as offerings by the people and the lowland farmers, and fetched them as needed by the Mission Housekeeper, and — when some got overripe and the Mission Housekeeper complained of the smell — it was up to him to weed out the bad and store the good so the air circulated around them.

In short, it was Mbasa Kilu's responsibility to do *any* job needed by Brother Jerome Jenkins, or requested by Sister Sheila

McMurphy, who was in charge of the brightly colored rugs made by the ladies and the sewing, or ordered by the Mission Housekeeper, Miss Rose, who was in charge of everything else, so that Brother Jerome Jenkins and Sister Sheila McMurphy were kept happy, and especially Miss Rose was kept happy, and the ladies could do their work and the Mission Center was kept at peace. This was the job of the Mission Caretaker, Mbasa Kilu.

And one other duty to be mentioned — *Drive the Brothers' Truck When Needed to Do Errands.* This duty was assigned only after Mbasa Kilu drove the Great Gasoline-Powered Lawn Mower for six months. And Brother Jerome Jenkins made several appeals to the manager of the local Federal Office over getting Mbasa Kilu the driving permit. He was finally persuasive when he mentioned that the manager of the regional government office — even though it was located in Brightwood Crossing — was a graduate of Maryville Regional Vocational High School and a long-time Douglastown fan, and it would be a shame if Mbasa Kilu, the equipment manager of the regional manager's favorite team, was unable to prepare properly for the next game — because the permit clerk at the Douglastown Federal Office had not yet issued a driving permit to Mbasa Kilu.

Needless to say, Mbasa Kilu then got the permit.

* * * * *

Now since the job of Mission Caretaker required Mbasa Kilu to live in the small apartment at the end of the Mission Center Annex, he moved out of Grandmother Nona's house for the first time in his life. She helped him furnish his apartment with a few things from her apartment. But he still lived close to her, and visited her, and once or twice a week had supper with her. And several times a week, he ate with the brothers. And sometimes, if he worked late, Miss Rose would leave a plate for him, and complain if he didn't wash it properly and replace it on the correct stack in her cupboard.

And even after he moved out, Mbasa Kilu continued to help Grandmother Nona by performing repairs in her house, like replacing a tube in her old TV set, or like repairing Brother Jerome Jenkins' old cordless remote phone and installing it for Grandmother Nona to use in her apartment. Though he could not seem to convince her — even when he demonstrated it

— that she could answer phone calls to her house by picking up the cordless remote phone. "Anyway," she said, "it's just two steps to reach the phone in the kitchen." So the cordless remote phone lay unused.

* * * * *

After the Mission had grown to where it occupied a good part of the former Imperial College, the men gathered to erect a chicken house for Brother Jerome Jenkins to keep the chickens, because more space was needed in the garage, and a library and a school cafeteria and a physics lab aren't the best place in the world for raising chickens. So the men erected chicken runs and tacked up chicken wire, just as Brother Jerome Jenkins directed them, and hauled wet concrete in the wheelbarrows for the slabs between, and so on. And they spent the better part of a Thursday and a Friday and a Saturday, almost until the sun went down, putting up this chicken house to make food and money for the Mission. And all day Thursday and Friday and Saturday the men worked — framing the chicken runs and tacking up the chicken wire and hauling wet concrete in the wheelbarrows.

Now Mbasa Kilu was not allowed to help with this, because they said he could hurt himself with the hammer, framing the chicken runs and tacking up the chicken wire, or hurt himself hauling wet concrete in the wheelbarrow. And didn't the men have enough to do? Working all day Thursday and Friday and Saturday? To get the job done before Sunday services? Without having to wait for Mbasa Kilu to finish a piece of chicken wire a fraction of the size of what any of them could do? Or to wait for him to haul a load of wet concrete a fraction of the size of what any one of them could haul?

Which is not the way Brother Jerome Jenkins put it, of course: he gave Mbasa Kilu the job of moving boxes and containers around and fetching things for the ladies who were busy in the kitchen of the Imperial College Faculty Club — now the residence of the Brothers of St. Columban — preparing pitchers of lemonade and trays of sandwiches for the workers.

Tedu Ngraeba clapped Mbasa Kilu on the back in thanks for helping, and kidded him not to be making time with the ladies in the kitchen while the men were all working, which caused all the men to laugh, including Mbasa Kilu and even Brother Jerome Jenkins, although after a while, when some of the men were still laughing among themselves, Mbasa Kilu wondered what it was about, if it was still Tedu Ngraeba's good joke? Or something else? And sure enough when Brother Jerome Jenkins and Tedu Ngraeba were not looking someone called him *Owasi Kilu,* which meant "wounded goat," instead of Mbasa Kilu, which meant "wild goat." And then pretended it was just a slip of the tongue, and not intentional, and not to be taken seriously, Mbasa Kilu, old boy, old man, don't lose your sense of humor.

And now that he was older, he had a question. If it was true — at least according to the men — that he was not able to help frame the chicken runs and nail up chicken wire and haul wet concrete for the slabs between, and was not able to take part with them in work or in football, then how come he was able to steer the Great Gasoline-Powered Lawn Mower over the vast lawn around the Mission Center Annex building, even on the terraces sloping toward the precipice overlooking the Great River? And how come he was able — by himself — to raise and lower the double garage doors at the end of the Annex building, which of course none of the ladies or for that matter no two of them were able to manage? And how come he was able to start up the brothers' truck and drive it to pick up light bulbs at the hardware out on Maryville Pike, avoiding for the most part the pot holes?

Mbasa Kilu even thought of going to Tedu Ngraeba and asking him these questions. But only in his mind did he ask Tedu Ngraeba these questions, because he knew what some claimed: that the Great Spirit, which avenged the sin of his father, would not allow him, Mbasa Kilu, to join the men in work or in football, to frame the chicken runs or nail up the chicken wire or haul the wet concrete. Even though he himself no longer believed the business of the vengeance of the Great Spirit, nor did Grandmother Nona believe it, nor did any of the White Franciscan Sisters. But to keep peace, he kept quiet about it, and accepted the job that was given him.

* * * * *

Brother Jerome Jenkins said there were also underground gasoline and diesel storage tanks at the Imperial Army ROTC Center, at the former Imperial College, which a contractor from Brightwood Crossing was supposed to dig up carefully and carry off to Brightwood Crossing to be cleansed and disposed of, because Brother Jerome Jenkins said they would cause damage to the soil, thus to the yams and the sugar beets and the drinking water. But on the day the contractor was to come from Brightwood Crossing, Brother Jerome Jenkins was called to a dying great-grandfather six towns away, and was not able to be there when the contractor came, so he told Mbasa Kilu the details of what the contractor's men were to do, and left him to oversee it.

Mbasa Kilu watched the contractor's men arrive in their trucks, and get off the trucks and sit in the shade, while the Contractor's Big Man, who wore a cap that said "Oakland Raiders," which Mbasa Kilu understood to be a U.S. football team, surveyed the site Brother Jerome Jenkins had designated as the site of the underground gasoline and diesel storage tanks, if there were in fact such tanks. And after he had surveyed the site the Contractor's Big Man spoke to Mbasa Kilu. He introduced himself as Tyler Zachary, and told him what they planned to do, and Mbasa Kilu spoke back to the Contractor's Big Man, in the baseball cap that said "Oakland Raiders," and told him about the damage Brother Jerome Jenkins said would happen to the soil, and the yams and sugar beets as well, and the drinking water. And he told the Contractor's Big Man how important it was to Brother Jerome Jenkins, who was six towns away giving a blessing to a great-grandfather, that the damage resulting from the underground gasoline and diesel storage tanks be prevented.

And Mbasa Kilu watched the Contractor's Big Man, in the Oakland Raiders cap, call the other men from the shade. And Mbasa Kilu watched them dig around in the soil at the spot where Brother Jerome Jenkins said the underground tanks were buried. And then Mbasa Kilu watched the men stop, and go back to the shade, and drink from their flasks. And then dig in the soil some more in a different spot, and then the flasks again, and the shade. And another spot, and so on and so on, until a large area was dug up, but only as deep as the length of your hand, like a garden for planting flowers. Then he watched the contractor's men bury Gndoro Juju medals in this garden to prevent the damage to the soil and allow the tanks to remain buried, without being ripped up and dragged clear to Brightwood Crossing. And after more shade and more drinking from the flasks, the contractor's men replaced the soil they had scraped away over a large area, and stomped it down with their feet.

And afterward the men knocked off for the night and since it was too late to return to Brightwood Crossing, they set up camp, some in their trucks, some on the lawn of the Mission Compound. And the contractor's men built a fire and cooked their supper right there and shared with Mbasa Kilu their flasks and their cooked chicken wings they brought along. And they drank from their flasks until after sundown, and built another fire, and killed and roasted another chicken, one that belonged to Brother Jerome Jenkins, and had not only wings but legs and breast as well, and drank from their flasks. And the Contractor's Big Man gave Mbasa Kilu the Oakland Raiders cap, and the contractor's men sang and danced around the fire, even Mbasa Kilu, who didn't dance well at all, and for that matter didn't sing very well either, but with the contractor's men sang and danced, until the contractor's men one by one fell asleep around the fire. First Mbasa Kilu was going to go to his bed in the rear of the Mission Center Annex building, but instead he too fell asleep beside the fire, on the ground along with the contractor's men.

And in the morning, the contractor's men got back in their truck, without the tanks, of course, which were left in the ground, and pointed *Good Health!* to Mbasa Kilu, and rode back to Brightwood Crossing, and Mbasa Kilu pointed *Good Health!* to the contractor's men, and tipped his Oakland Raiders baseball cap to the Contractor's Big Man, and waved to them as they drove off.

Later in the day when Brother Jerome Jenkins came back from six towns away, where he had blessed the dying grandfather, he stopped at the Mission Center Annex building to ask about the work. And Mbasa Kilu showed him the wide area where the contractor's men had dug, but, of course, did not tell him of the buried Gndoro Juju medals to prevent the damage to the soil, even without digging up the tanks and dragging them clear to Brightwood Crossing to be disposed of.

The next day when Brother Jerome Jenkins asked about the missing chicken, Mbasa Kilu showed him a break in the fence where the chicken could have slipped out.

* * * * *

Now the rug and sewing ladies paid not much attention to Mbasa Kilu, except now and then when a storm came up in the middle of the day, and they needed the double garage doors at the end of the Annex building put down, so that the rains would not sweep in and ruin their rugs, and the winds would not tip the great looms over. Mbasa Kilu, for his part, went about his business, and steered the Great Gasoline-Powered Lawn Mower around the vast lawn surrounding the Annex building, and gathered eggs, and did the jobs set out for him by Brother Jerome Jenkins, such as patch the spot in the fence so that the chickens would not slip out.

His routine was slightly different on sewing days, when the looms and brightly colored rugs were set aside for the day, and Sister Sheila McMurphy came and taught the ladies about clothing, and how to set up the sewing machines, how to operate the sewing machines, where to cut, where to sew, how to gather up the waist, how to taper the shoulders properly, and so on.

Mbasa Kilu knew when there was to be sewing day, because he saw Sister Sheila McMurphy arrive, very early, and because it was his job, before the ladies began to gather, to move aside two of the huge looms, leaving room to set up the sewing machines, which Sister Sheila McMurphy did *not* want Mbasa Kilu to do, she said, because she wanted the ladies to learn how.

And on sewing day Mbasa Kilu saw the ladies trying on clothing they had made. And they laughed and clapped over the clothing, dresses like Sister Sheila McMurphy wore. And he considered what if one of these ladies was his wife, and if he had a house for her like the Chief Onyaka Nwilu. What fine things they could do together, and what fine children they would have, better than all the children of the Chief Onyaka Nwilu, children without their feet turned in, children whose ankles were not bent, children who could laugh and sing, and play football.

And every time there was sewing day, Mbasa Kilu thought the ladies were especially beautiful, not only in the dresses they made, but perhaps even more so in the *luyaàs* they wore when not in their blue uniforms. And he thought this especially about the girl Ofi Leiya, who once went with Mbasa Kilu to the same grade of the White Franciscan Sisters' School, where she helped him with his spelling words; Ofi Leiya, who in the cafeteria at the Maryville Regional Vocational High School sometimes set her tray down beside his, when her friends and admirers were not crowding around her, and — when he had to give a speech in class — encouraged him to speak from his heart.

And sometimes when the ladies left, Mbasa Kilu watched them from the lawn, and watched Ofi Leiya, and considered how happy he would be if she were his wife, and what fine things they would do together, and what fine children they would have together, children better even than those of the Chief Onyaka Nwilu, children whose feet were not turned in, and whose ankles were not bent. Children who could sing and dance and play football.

And in his imagination Mbasa Kilu asked Ofi Leiya to be his wife, and have fine children with him. But in reality he only watched for Ofi Leiya at a distance, and remembered the spelling words, and her tray beside his in the cafeteria, and speaking from the heart, and so on. Because in reality Mbasa Kilu knew that at the Mission Picnic Ofi Leiya danced with Tedu Ngraeba, captain of the men's football team, who had been the tallest boy at the White Franciscan Sisters' School, and carried the gold cross at the head of processions, and now was big and tall and strong as a man, and able to dig paths and irrigation ditches, and able to frame chicken runs and nail up the chicken wire and haul the greatest load of wet concrete for the slabs between.

And in reality Mbasa Kilu saw that his own feet were turned in and his ankles bent, that when he walked he wobbled from one side to the other. He knew he would not be able to be like Tedu Ngraeba, would not be able to dance with Ofi Leiya at the Mission Picnic, and above all would not be able to have Ofi Leiya for his bride, would not be able to have fine children with her, children with their feet turned to the front, and their ankles straight, children who could sing and dance and play football.

* * * * *

Even though Mbasa Kilu no longer believed in the vengeance of the Great Spirit, he realized that his feet were what they were. He realized that his steps were wobbly. Even though his Grandmother Nona said what a handsome man he was, and even though Glynnis, her friend next door, greeted him "hey, good looking" and pretended to want to court him, he knew how he had appeared to the girls at school, where only Ofi Leiya ever put her tray down beside his at lunch time. He knew how he appeared to the girls in the sewing class, who would come out into the courtyard on their break, and sometimes speak to him if he were nearby, but not stay to share any stories or laughs with him. He knew how he appeared to the girls at the Mission dances. When he first showed up at one of the dances, the girls tried not to let him see them staring at his feet (which they did, and which he saw) and they were careful to avoid eye contact with him. And if he even walked in their direction, the girls were quick to gather their purses and head for the rest room, or for the refreshment area for another Royal Crown Cola.

So he just stopped coming to the Mission dances. Except to pretend he had some official duty, like emptying the trash barrels, or carrying another case of Royal Crown Cola to the refreshment area — which he did sometimes just to see who was at the dance. And mainly to see if Ofi Leiya was there, and to get a glimpse of her dancing, which she would be, with his friend Tedu Ngraeba.

Before leaving he would sometimes stop at the food table and get a slice of mango or a biscuit. And after he saw what he saw, and ate what he ate, he would leave, escaping the embarrassment of the staring and avoiding.

* * * * *

Now in the last moon before the rains every three years, the Archbishop came for Visitation. Visitation was only for a few days, but many days before were required to prepare. There was much time spent by the cooks and *gnokos* tending the fires where extra chickens and yams and even a pig were roasted, to prepare for the Visitation. And there was much steering of the Great Gasoline-Powered Lawn Mower over the vast lawn of the Mission Compound. And many extra jobs set out for Mbasa Kilu by Brother Jerome Jenkins, not only patching all the fences, not only polishing the windows of the Mission Center Annex building, but painting the flagpoles in the compound. Also he painted the wind direction indicator and navigation aids at the airstrip, and marked the runway with lime. For the Archbishop came all the way from Indoniva, across the mountains on the other coast, and flew his own plane and landed right there at the airstrip.

The day the Archbishop arrived, the people gathered at the airstrip and waved their flags, and the Archbishop landed his plane, and those who were the best singers and dancers sang and danced, and they marched in a parade to the center of the Mission Compound, where the cooks and the *gnokos* had prepared the large fire, and there the chickens and yams were eaten, and even the pig and all the mangos and choleas which had been gathered, and everyone drank only of the grape drink prepared by the ladies, not of the flasks, which the men kept hidden in their pockets. And after this fine feast, the Archbishop retired to Brother Jerome Jenkins's house to start the Visitation. Because in addition to the singers and dancers and polished windows, and the chickens and yams, and even the pig, and the grape drink, which the cooks and *gnokos* and the ladies had prepared for the Visitation, in addition to all this, the Mission Secretary had typed many sheets for Brother Jerome Jenkins, to tell the Archbishop the story of the Mission for the last three years, to count for him the number of training classes which had been held, the number of home visits which had been made, the number of senior-citizen lunches which had been served, and so on and so on. And Mbasa Kilu sometimes imagined that the sheets the Mission Secretary typed even told of the number of yams and sugar beets he had put aside in the loft of the garage and the number of times he had run the Great Gasoline-Powered Lawn Mower over the lawns and the terraces, though he didn't really think so.

And while the Archbishop heard the story, and read it, the men of the village drifted off to the road outside the Mission Compound, near the precipice overlooking the Great River, and shared the flasks which they could not share inside the Mission Center during the celebration of the singers and dancers and polished windows, and the chickens and yams.

* * * * *

And the next morning when the sun was up, before Brother Jerome Jenkins and the Archbishop emerged from the house, Mbasa Kilu rose and opened the double garage doors and lined up the looms, all but two of them, because today would be a day at the looms, for rugs, but also a sewing day, and Sister Sheila McMurphy would be there, and the ladies would wear their best *luyaàs*, and they would run the looms, and make rugs, but also they would show they knew how to set up the sewing machines, how to operate the sewing machines, where to cut, where to sew, how to gather up the waist, how to taper the shoulders properly, and so on. And they would show on hangers the dresses they made, dresses like Sister Sheila McMurphy wore. And they would wear their best *luyaàs*, which they wore especially for the Visitation.

And after the Archbishop had seen the looms, and seen the ladies making a rug, and admired their beautiful rugs, and seen the ladies set up the sewing machines, seen them *operate* the sewing machines, and seen the dresses they held up for him, dresses like Sister Sheila McMurphy wore, and after the Archbishop talked to the ladies, and told them how pleased he was, and after they laughed and clapped for him — after all this he and Brother Jerome Jenkins came outside again through the double garage doors at the end of the Annex building, and Mbasa Kilu thought they would go to Brother Jerome Jenkins's house again, to hear more of the story of the people that the Mission Secretary had typed.

But instead they left the path and walked onto the vast lawn, around the side of the Annex building to where Mbasa Kilu waited in case a wind or a rain blew up, requiring the double garage doors to be closed, or in case there appeared a spot on the polished windows that needed to be wiped away before the Archbishop saw it.

And Brother Jerome Jenkins walked straight toward Mbasa Kilu, and addressed him directly, and told the Archbishop that this was Mbasa Kilu. "This is the Mission Caretaker I spoke of last night," said Brother Jerome Jenkins.

And the Archbishop held out his hand to Mbasa Kilu, and Mbasa Kilu shook it. And the Archbishop smiled, and Brother Jerome Jenkins smiled, and Mbasa Kilu tried to smile. But he was puzzled about why the Archbishop and Brother Jerome Jenkins approached him, for there was no wind or rain requiring the doors to be shut, and if there were spots on the polished windows it was too late to get them, for the Archbishop was right here before him. And Mbasa Kilu did not know what was required of him.

The Archbishop said something to Mbasa Kilu he did not understand, and when he still looked puzzled Brother Jerome

Jenkins explained that the Archbishop wished him well. And Mbasa Kilu smiled. "The Archbishop wants to help you with your feet turned in, and your bent ankles," said Brother Jerome Jenkins. And Mbasa Kilu did not understand, and looked puzzled again. And Brother Jerome Jenkins went on. The Archbishop lived in Indoniva, across the mountains on the other coast, said Brother Jerome Jenkins. And in Indoniva, said Brother Jerome Jenkins, there was a hospital.

And when Mbasa Kilu heard the word "hospital," he thought of the trips to the clinics of the Maryville Region when he was 11 and 12, cab fare paid both ways, and of the drive to Brightwood Crossing with the White Franciscan Nurse Sister. And he knew that none of the doctors and nurses were able to help him, not even the White Franciscan Nurse Sister, who was considered the top nurse in Douglastown, and for that matter in the entire Maryville Region. And Mbasa Kilu did not know how to explain this to Brother Jerome Jenkins, without embarrassing him in front of his boss the Archbishop, so Mbasa Kilu pretended to be confused.

And when Brother Jerome Jenkins saw Mbasa Kilu confused, he took his time and explained to Mbasa Kilu. And Brother Jerome Jenkins said a Big Doctor was coming to the hospital in Indoniva, who knew how to help people whose feet were turned in, and whose ankles were bent. Mbasa Kilu smiled, because he could not imagine a doctor helping him. But he was patient, and he respected Brother Jerome Jenkins, and especially did not want to cause embarrassment to Brother Jerome Jenkins in front of his boss the Archbishop, in the middle of Visitation, so he listened, and smiled, and listened, and was puzzled, and listened, until Brother Jerome Jenkins finally explained to him the full story of the Big Doctor who helped people with their feet turned in and their ankles bent. This Big Doctor was able to cut away the illness of the feet and the ankles, so that the feet would be turned straight, and the ankles not bent. And this cutting away of the illness was called surgery. And Mbasa Kilu listened as Brother Jerome Jenkins explained to him that Mbasa Kilu could get in the plane with the Archbishop, and fly back to Indoniva, where the Archbishop would take Mbasa Kilu to the hospital, and the Big Doctor would cut away the illness of Mbasa Kilu's feet and ankles, so that when they healed from the surgery Mbasa Kilu's feet would be turned straight and his ankles not bent.

Now Mbasa Kilu knew about surgery, of course, not only from CNN *Medical Update* but because of Jennifer on *Every Woman's Love*, who of course ended up having surgery on the day she was to have married Lance. But CNN was one thing, Jennifer on *Every Woman's Love* was one thing. The Great Spirit was something else. Mbasa Kilu worried that it might not be possible through the help of even the Biggest Doctor to reverse that which the Great Spirit had done to him to avenge the sin of his father — even though Grandmother Nona had told him not to believe this. But he did not want to embarrass Brother Jerome Jenkins in front of his boss the Archbishop during Visitation, so he smiled, and he asked him, "Who will be Mission Caretaker while I have surgery?"

And Brother Jerome Jenkins smiled, and the Archbishop smiled. And Brother Jerome Jenkins said, "Who do you want to be Mission Caretaker?"

And Mbasa Kilu said, "Mission Caretaker is *my* job."

And Brother Jerome Jenkins said, "Yes, it is your job. But in order to go to Indoniva, to have the Big Doctor do the surgery to cure the illness of your feet and ankles, you must set aside the job of Mission Caretaker. Joroi Urkundi will become Mission Caretaker." Now Mbasa Kilu knew that Joroi Urkundi was a man with seven grandchildren. When he was younger, he worked in the fields and chopped yams and hunted pigs and even cut paths for the people to walk on and dug irrigation ditches bringing water to the crops. But now Joroi Urkundi suffered from an illness of the knees and hips which made it difficult for him to chop yams and made him too slow to hunt pigs and made it impossible for him to dig paths for the people, much less irrigation ditches for the crops.

"How will Joroi Urkundi — with his illness of the hips and knees — raise the huge garage doors at the end of the Mission Center Annex building?" asked Mbasa Kilu.

And Brother Jerome Jenkins smiled and started to explain, but the Archbishop put a hand on Brother Jerome Jenkins's arm, and said something to Brother Jerome Jenkins that Mbasa Kilu did not understand, and Brother Jerome Jenkins said to the Archbishop, "You're right, Archbishop, I didn't think of that." And he said to Mbasa Kilu, "Mbasa Kilu, this is a wonderful opportunity for you, but you need time to think about it. Think it over, and think of all the questions you have, and I will answer them for you before three days. In three days the Archbishop flies back to Indoniva. You can fly with him. The Big Doctor in Indoniva will perform the surgery and cure your illness. Your feet will be set right, and your ankles not bent."

And Mbasa Kilu nodded, and kept silent about his doubts. For he knew Brother Jerome Jenkins believed the Big Doctor could do this, with the help of the Holy Spirit, whom Brother Jerome Jenkins believed and the White Franciscan Sisters taught was even greater than the Great Spirit.

And once again the Archbishop gave Mbasa Kilu his hand, and Mbasa Kilu shook it. And he tipped his Oakland Raiders baseball hat to the Archbishop, and the Archbishop smiled and waved back. Then the Archbishop and Brother Jerome Jenkins walked off toward Brother Jerome Jenkins's house, to read more of the sheets typed up by the Mission Secretary.

* * * * *

So Mbasa Kilu did as Brother Jerome Jenkins suggested, and began to think up all the questions he could about flying in the Archbishop's plane back to Indoniva, and all the questions about the Big Doctor and the surgery, and the questions about his illness, and so on, and how the surgery would make it so that his feet would not be turned in, and his ankles not bent.

The first questions he thought of were about Joroi Urkundi, and how he would assume the duties of Mission Caretaker, with his illness of the hips and knees. But as he thought of these questions he realized he himself would not be around to witness Joroi Urkundi as the Mission Caretaker, but would be in Indoniva with the Archbishop, visiting the Big Doctor who performed the surgery. So he put Joroi Urkundi aside and thought of other questions. But mostly they were questions Brother Jerome Jenkins would not be able to answer. For example, if he went to Indoniva and had the healing surgery to cure his feet and make his ankles not bent, would he be able to play football with the men of the village?

Would he be able to take the field beside Tedu Ngraeba, take the pass from him, make the winning shot on goal against Harbourtown? Would he be interviewed by Ofi Leiya for KXR13-TV? Would she ask him *How Do You Feel About This Victory, Mbasa Kilu?* Would he write his memoirs? Play the role of himself in a TV miniseries? Would his memoirs be placed on the shelf in the library beside the biographies of Brigadier General Solomon Gambwizi and President Robert Kloboso, both now dead, and *Profiles in Courage,* by President John F. Kennedy of the U.S.A., also now dead?

And for the answer to his first question, the question of football, he went to Tedu Ngraeba, now the captain of the Douglastown Leopards football team, who ran from the mid-fielder position. And Mbasa Kilu tipped his Oakland Raiders baseball cap, and said what a good day it was, and how nice the sun felt, and how well the Visitation with the Archbishop was going, and what a good party for the Archbishop, and how delicious the roast pig and the yams, and so on and so on. And he told Tedu about the Archbishop's offer to take him to see the Big Doctor and get the surgery. "Tedu Ngraeba," he said, "if the Big Doctor performs the surgery and cures the illness of my feet and ankles, will I be able to play football with the men of the village? Will I be able to kick the ball, in a real game, on the pitch, and not just on the sidelines? Will I be able to try out for the Douglastown Leopards?"

Tedu Ngraeba looked at him puzzled, then said: "Mbasa Kilu, my friend, man, the Great Spirit has twisted your feet and ankles since birth. I am sorry, Mbasa Kilu, my friend, man, but there is no healing from this Great Misfortune. There is no Big Doctor, no medicine, no cutting away of the illness, no surgery to cure what the Great Spirit has done in vengeance. Know what I mean, man?"

Mbasa Kilu did not really believe this about vengeance, but he knew Tedu Ngraeba was brought up believing it. And even though the White Franciscan Sisters taught the love of the Holy Spirit, not the vengeance of the Great Spirit, he knew it was hard to ignore what you have all your life been taught to believe. Which is why Tedu Ngraeba believed it — not because he was mean. So Mbasa Kilu was patient, and he listened to Tedu Ngraeba, and he answered him, and he explained about the Archbishop, and the Big Doctor, and the surgery that would cut away the illness of his feet and ankles, if he would fly back to Indoniva with the Archbishop.

Still Tedu Ngraeba was puzzled, and talked about the Great Spirit, and told Mbasa Kilu about the Great Spirit's revenge, and so on. And still Mbasa Kilu was patient, but persistent, and explained again and again about the Big Doctor and the surgery and the healing of his illness, and so on.

Finally Tedu Ngraeba drew himself up to his full height, so that Mbasa Kilu, with his feet bent under, barely reached Tedu Ngraeba's chest. And Tedu Ngraeba said, "Man, Mbasa Kilu, my friend, you want to play football? So what position do you play?"

Now Mbasa Kilu knew every position, knew which of the village men had played what position for the Douglastown Leopards as far back as when he was 7 years old. But though he knew all this, he himself had never played football, of course, because of his ankles bent and his feet turned in. So he was not able to answer Tedu Ngraeba. There was no position he knew how to play.

And Tedu Ngraeba said to him, "Man, that's it. That's it, my friend, Mbasa Kilu, man. In football, you have to play a position. If you play no position, how can you play football? How can you be in a game on the pitch? How can you try out for the Douglastown Leopards?" So that was the answer to the football question.

* * * * *

But there was also the other question, the question of Ofi Leiya. If he went to Indoniva with the Archbishop, and if the Big Doctor in Indoniva performed the surgery on his feet and ankles and cut away the illness — if this happened, would Ofi Leiya's eyes open to him in a different way? Could he dance with Ofi Leiya at the village dances? Could he court Ofi Leiya? Could he ask her to go on dates with him to the drugstore? Could he some day ask her to marry him, and do fine things with him, and have fine children, better even than those of the Great Chief Onyaka Nwilu? And Brother Jerome Jenkins, of course, was not the one to answer *this* question.

Nor could he ask Ofi Leiya such questions — at least not directly. Not the question of dances and dates. Nor — God forbid! — the questions of courtship and marriage. He would *never* ask Ofi Leiya those questions directly. Instead, he would ask her opinion, not about herself, but about other girls. If his feet and ankles were cured by the surgery, would *they* — the other girls, girls in general — look at him differently? Could he dance with them, go on dates with them? Eventually, could he court them, even ask one of them to be his wife? Though, in reality, he admitted that Ofi Leiya was the only girl who had ever paid attention to him, who had not ignored him. And, he admitted to himself, it was not the other girls in whom he was interested. It was Ofi Leiya.

So the day after he talked to Tedu Ngraeba, Mbasa Kilu waited outside the Annex building at noon, waited until the sound of the looms stopped, when he knew the ladies were about to take their lunch break. And Mbasa Kilu waited outside until Ofi Leiya walked out, laughing and clapping with two of her friends. Mbasa Kilu saw her notice him and give a little wave with her fingers, but she did not stop to talk, but walked on past with her friends, so that he had to follow her. When he caught up with Ofi Leiya and her friends, and they noticed him, they stopped laughing and talking and clapping, and waited to see what he was about. And Mbasa Kilu, as usual, was self-conscious in front of Ofi Leiya and her friends, and he tipped his Oakland Raiders cap, but didn't know the right words, so he said that he had a question for her. So Ofi Leiya turned to her friends, and they quietly walked away, and then she turned to Mbasa Kilu, to see what would be the question.

The easier part, which he got through okay, was to tell her about the Archbishop's offer to take him to see the Big Doctor in Indoniva and the surgery and the healing. Then he was self-conscious, and took off his Oakland Raiders baseball cap, and held it, and didn't know the right words, and he said the words that came to his lips, about the spelling words at the White Franciscan Sisters' School, and about the cafeteria at the Maryville Regional Vocational High School, and speaking from the heart, and so on and so on. Mostly he wanted to talk about the healing, and his feet not turned in, and his ankles not bent, but that part seemed to slip past his lips before he knew it, and before he knew it he came to the truly hard part. And three times he started with the truly hard part, and three times his lips failed him, and he started again. But finally he took a deep breath, and held his Oakland Raiders baseball cap in both hands, and blurted out the truly hard part.

"If I come back after the surgery," Mbasa Kilu said to Ofi Leiya, trying to face her, but too self-conscious to look into her eyes, the eyes of this girl, now no longer a girl but a woman. "If I come back to the village after the surgery, and my feet are no longer turned in, and my ankles are not bent," he said, and stumbled again. And here he meant to talk about dancing and courting and going on dates to the drugstore, and he meant to talk about girls in general, not Ofi Leiya, but his heart was beating and he forgot the right words. "If my feet are no longer turned in," he said to Ofi Leiya, "will you think differently about me?"

As soon as he said it he realized he had gotten it wrong, and had said "you," that he had forgotten to make it about the other girls, about girls in general. And he was embarrassed at the way it came out, and tried to correct it. "Girls," he said, "Will *they* think differently? At dances, for example." And he felt himself blushing, knowing that Ofi Leiya was who he really meant, that what he originally blurted out was the real truth, the real question he had.

And Ofi Leiya looked at him, then looked down at her own feet and ankles. And finally she looked up at him again.

"Mbasa Kilu," she said, "I don't know what they will think. I have seen them ignore you in the hallway at school; I have seen them walk away at dances; and I can't understand it. I don't think they have given themselves an opportunity to know you."

She talked about when they were young, at the White Franciscan Sisters' School, and about the spelling words. "I have known you since I was nine," she said. "I always thought you were brave to come to school and come to class — in spite of getting started late, in spite of the trouble walking. I have seen how clever you are. I have seen how bright you are, in spite of your late start in school. I have seen how good you do every job you are given. I have seen how honest you are. Surgery or no surgery, I think you are a good man. I think someday you will make a good husband and a good father."

And Mbasa Kilu was taken aback to hear Ofi Leiya say this about him — even though he was sure Ofi Leiya meant a good husband to some *other* girl. But since the fat was already in the fire, so to speak, and just to be sure, he looked now directly into Ofi Leiya's eyes and asked her if she had promised marriage to someone else. And she nodded her head yes.

"Tedu Ngraeba?" said Mbasa Kilu. And she nodded her head yes.

* * * * *

After the conversation with Ofi Leiya, Mbasa Kilu felt disappointed, completely empty, but not really surprised. Did he ever really believe that any surgery could change how he had been looked at ever since those first days, walking up the front sidewalk of school from the white van, having the gesture of *Not-Right-in-the-Head* made behind his back?

Nevertheless, there was one last question Mbasa Kilu thought of, one Brother Jerome Jenkins could answer, and he saved it until he saw Brother Jerome Jenkins the night before the Archbishop left. Actually Mbasa Kilu thought of the question when he thought of Joroi Urkundi, the grandfather of seven with the illness of the knees and hips who was to take his place as Mission Caretaker during the time he was in Indoniva, with the Archbishop and the Big Doctor. And he thought of the question, What will Joroi Urkundi do when he, Mbasa Kilu, returns from Indoniva after the surgery and after the healing? And as he thought of the question he realized it was the wrong question, that the real question was: Would he, Mbasa Kilu, be Mission Caretaker when he returned? Would he be the person to steer the Great Gasoline-Powered Lawn Mower over the great slopes? Over the lawns and the terraces of the Mission Compound?

And when Mbasa Kilu asked this question, Brother Jerome Jenkins first looked at him surprised. Then Brother Jerome Jenkins laughed and clapped him on the shoulder. "Mbasa Kilu, when you return from Indoniva after the surgery and after your feet have healed, you won't *have* to be Mission Caretaker," said Brother Jerome Jenkins. "First of all, we would have Joroi Urkundi. Secondly, your feet will be straight, and your ankles no longer bent. Mbasa Kilu, when you return from Indoniva you will be whatever you want!"

And now Brother Jerome Jenkins too looked worried, but with both hands he clapped Mbasa Kilu on *both* shoulders, and smiled at him, and tried to reassure him. "Everything will work out well, Mbasa Kilu. Tonight before you go to sleep you will pack your toothbrush and razor, and extra underwear. And tomorrow morning you will get to the airstrip on time. And you will fly to Indoniva with the Archbishop. And the Big Doctor will perform the surgery on your feet and ankles, and there will be healing. And after the surgery and after your feet have healed you will be home again, and your feet will no longer be turned in, and your ankles will be straight." And Brother Jerome Jenkins clapped him on the shoulders again, and smiled again.

But Mbasa Kilu was silent. Because Mbasa Kilu knew that Brother Jerome Jenkins believed in the love of the Holy Spirit, which he believed would help the Big Doctor perform the surgery and the healing. And even though Mbasa Kilu was taught the love of the Holy Spirit and so on by the White Franciscan Sisters, he still sometimes wondered if the Holy Spirit could really love him enough to take away the great misfortune of his feet and ankles. So Mbasa Kilu knew there were no more questions for Brother Jerome Jenkins, and Mbasa Kilu was silent.

* * * * *

Next morning the people of the village gathered again at the airstrip for the Archbishop's plane to take off. The markers and navigation aids and wind direction indicator were bright with the paint applied by Mbasa Kilu, the Mission Caretaker, and the lime still marked the runway lines that the Archbishop could use taking off. And those who could dance, danced; and those who could sing, sang. And everyone waved flags as the Archbishop arrived at the airstrip, certainly to please the Archbishop, but also because the Visitation was over for another three years, and the ladies did not have to do the looms and the sewing both on one day, and the men did not have to be as careful to keep the flasks hidden away from the Mission Compound, close to the Great River, and life could go back to normal.

And when Brother Jerome Jenkins and the Archbishop saw Mbasa Kilu, he was in his regular work clothes, and his Oakland Raiders cap, having put up the double garage doors at six a.m., as usual. Moreover, Mbasa Kilu had no suitcase, no laundry bag even, containing his toothbrush and razor and extra underwear, his things for the trip to Indoniva.

And Brother Jerome Jenkins became excited, and he started to gesture and tell Mbasa Kilu what to do, but the Archbishop put his hand on Brother Jerome Jenkins's arm, to calm him down. And the Archbishop looked Mbasa Kilu in the eye, and said something Mbasa Kilu did not completely understand, though he thought he knew what it was. And Brother Jerome Jenkins repeated it for him.

"The Archbishop wants to know," Brother Jerome Jenkins said, "if all of your questions about the trip to Indoniva, and the Big Doctor, and the surgery, and the healing of your feet and ankles, have been answered?" And Mbasa Kilu nodded his head yes. "And the Archbishop wants to know," said Brother Jerome Jenkins, "if you have decided what to do?" And Mbasa Kilu nodded his head yes. "And will you go with the Archbishop?" said Brother Jerome Jenkins. And Mbasa Kilu shook his head no.

And even though the Archbishop understood, Brother Jerome Jenkins explained it to him, and repeated Mbasa Kilu's answers. And Brother Jerome Jenkins's face was red, and Mbasa Kilu was sorry for embarrassing him in front of his boss the Archbishop.

But the Archbishop was calm, and understood, and looked at Mbasa Kilu, and put a hand on his head. Then he pointed *Good Health!* to Mbasa Kilu, and he and Mbasa Kilu shook hands a last time.

And after that people sang and danced and waved flags, and Mbasa Kilu tipped his Oakland Raiders baseball cap, and the Archbishop waved back, and gave his blessing again and again from the steps of the plane. And then the Archbishop climbed into the cockpit, started the engine, and checked the direction signals and the white navigation aids, recently repainted by the Mission Caretaker, Mbasa Kilu, and steered the plane down the runway between the white lines, and took off for Indoniva.

And so for Mbasa Kilu there was no trip to Indoniva, and instead he returned to the Mission Compound, and started the engine of the Great Gasoline-Powered Lawn Mower, even though the lawn had been tended just a few days before. And Mbasa Kilu steered the Great Gasoline-Powered Lawn Mower around and around the lawn, along the fences surrounding the yard where the chickens spent the day, around the garage in whose loft the yams and sugar beets were stored, along the wall of the Mission Center Annex building, where the looms were already humming again and the ladies already returned to work, weaving the brightly colored rugs. And Mbasa Kilu steered the Great Gasoline-Powered Lawn Mower even onto the terraces sloping down to the precipice overlooking the Great River, which roared through the gorge, clearing everything in its path.

Section 2 — What a Young Life!

Tedu Ngraeba was Mbasa Kilu's friend and protector from the early days at the White Franciscan Sisters' school. He was a famous person when he died, too young. But, first, the fame.

Even as a student at Maryville Regional Vocational High School, Tedu Ngraeba excelled. By the time he graduated, he was already famous. On the very day of his graduation, he was awarded the Brother Josephus medal for outstanding Leadership in Athletics and Academics, for having an excellent record in his school work and for having scored more goals than any other player ever at Maryville Regional Vocational High School. *Twice* the number of goals. Mbasa Kilu could quote the exact numbers — of goals, of assists, of minutes played — everything! Had anyone before even come close to posting such numbers? Didn't that tell everyone what to expect of Tedu Ngraeba, playing from the midfielder position for the Douglastown Leopards? Didn't everyone know, even before Tedu Ngraeba put on the Gold and Black jersey of the Douglastown Leopards, that one record after another would be broken, that Tedu Ngraeba's whole life would be a record? Oh, the sadness of it! What a record! What a young life!

His first year after High School, his first year with the Douglastown Leopards, awarded the medal for Best New Player of the Year. That same year, selected to Second Team All League, kept from first team only by the performance of that other great midfielder, the great Jimbo Akaya himself, now a great veteran player. That year Douglastown had a winning record for the first time in 17 years and almost made it to the playoffs.

His second season, Tedu Ngraeba was again forced to play in the shadow of the great Jimbo Akaya, a long-time all star and great veteran player. Nevertheless Tedu Ngraeba led his team to a playoff in which they were narrowly defeated for the championship of the entire Continental Football League, some say because the referees were chosen from the province of Dunstan, one even from the town of Mount Elliott, which was the home team and the defending champion and thus the site of the championship playoff. But who can blame the referees, with forty-five thousand in the stands, all from Dunstan province, screaming for a Mount Elliott victory, and another one-hundred thousand (also from Dunstan Province) milling about the nearby fields and pastures, many not knowing the progress of the game but only the mood of the crowd they were with and the feel of the flasks in their hands, between their lips, the warm liquid in their throats and stomachs, and their own excitement and rage, many indulging frequently in the flasks, which they didn't even pretend to keep hidden from the police, of which there were far too few. So Tedu Ngraeba was denied the championship necklace for the second year.

But the next year, following the retirement of the great Jimbo Akaya (now a renowned former player, though still alive), Tedu Ngraeba and the Douglastown Leopards advanced to the finals of the playoffs and won so decisively that even referees born and raised in Dunstan Province, even in the very town of Mount Elliott, were not sufficient to swing the outcome the other way. And that year also there were forty-five thousand screaming fans in the grandstand and one-hundred thousand others milling about the fields and pastures, frequently partaking of the flasks. By the end of the match, they directed their screams and their anger at the home team, losing here on their home field in disgrace, following the retirement of the great Jimbo Akaya. And in fact the last two minutes of the final game were abandoned as fans poured onto the field and the players and coaches of the home team, playing for the first year without the services of the great Jimbo Akaya, ran for the parking lot, tearing off their green and yellow jerseys on the way, while the Douglastown Leopards and Tedu Ngraeba, Captain and midfielder, stood in confusion as fans ran past them, until they too took refuge in their team bus and headed back for the Maryville Province, leaving the championship trophy lying on the sidelines where it had been knocked from the presentation stand by stampeding fans.

The following year the Douglastown Leopards, with Tedu Ngraeba as team captain and starting midfielder, not only went to the finals of the Continental Football League Playoff, now on their home turf, but won decisively. In the process they toppled one team after another, even on the other team's home field, during the regular season. They beat the hated Mount Elliott Lions, first in the regular season, on the Mount Elliott field, then at home in the playoffs. They advanced to the championship game against Sherbourne City, who had been championship threats regularly in the days before the coming to prominence of the great Jimbo Akaya, then the league's greatest midfielder, now a renowned retired midfielder, who led Mount Elliott to the championship four straight years.

But Sherbourne City that year was not as good as the team of the past, and the Douglastown Leopards swept past them like one more small bump in the road on the way to the championship. Before intermission Douglastown put up a two-goal lead on goals by Tedu Ngraeba. Then — when the helpless Sherbourne City defense triple-teamed him in the second period — Tedu Ngraeba repeatedly passed to open teammates who kept the Sherbourne City goaltender busy.

And then the team stood proudly on the presentation stand to receive the championship trophy, with police reinforcements lining the field on both sides, but not needed this year, as fans also stood proudly and cheered and sang again and again *Dance, Joyful Leopards, Dance!* fight song of the Douglastown Leopards, then cheered and sang and danced themselves as Tedu Ngraeba stepped forward to receive the championship trophy, and then stepped forward again to have placed around his neck his reward for being the outstanding player of the season — the Gold Medal and Orange and Blue ribbon of the *Grand Prix de Jacques Rondebal,* named of course after the venerable founder of the Continental Football League. How can anyone remember such a scene, how can anyone remember this, the fame of Tedu Ngraeba, without shedding a tear?

* * * * *

By the following season — with two championships to his credit and another predicted — Tedu Ngraeba would play the championship match in front of Mr. Raymond Perotta, friend of Brother James Connelly since they attended both high school and college together in the U.S. Now Mr. Raymond Perotta was also a renowned sports agent from the U.S., who combined his visits to Brother James Connelly with his scouting trips around the UEFA Champions League in Europe, looking for NFL prospects for the U.S. — NFL being the U.S. equivalent of the Champions League, except the game being played is U.S. football, considered by many to be a joke and an object of ridicule, not real football. Mbasa Kilu had watched U.S. football on ESPN with the brothers, who were avid fans — at least those from the U.S. It was a game in which players were active only a few seconds at a time, threw the ball with their hands, knocked each other down, then lined up, and huddled, and played another few seconds, threw the ball with their hands, or held the ball while they ran, then knocked each other down, and so on. Nevertheless, NFL football paid high salaries to its players, though not as high as salaries paid to those in the U.S. who wrecked the world financial system — and this too was a joke on the U.S. and an object of ridicule.

But Brother James Connelly had invited Mr. Raymond Perotta to the game, and Coach Luke Omayinka ordered the players to treat him with respect. There were to be no jokes about U.S. football; no jokes about the U.S.

Mr. Raymond Perotta appeared for the first time the Thursday before the championship match was played on Sunday. It was widely thought that Mr. Raymond Perotta was there to scout Tedu Ngraeba for American football — something which had never been done before: a Continental Football League player, playing U.S. football.

Mbasa Kilu himself thought there was a possibility Mr. Raymond Perotta would sign Tedu Ngraeba to a high-paying contract in the U.S. Although Mbasa Kilu wished him luck, he couldn't imagine what life would be like without Tedu Ngraeba and Ofi Leiya.

As for Mr. Raymond Perotta, he was there to visit Brother James Connelly, his high school and college friend, not to scout the Continental Football League, which was several steps below the Champions League, which he had already scouted. But that didn't keep the people of Douglastown from thinking what they wanted to think, from hoping what they wanted to hope.

The air was already thick with the excitement of the championship match, the anticipation of another Douglastown victory, when a taxi from Sherbourne City discharged Mr. Raymond Perotta and his luggage in the courtyard of the compound. Brother James Connelly had been waiting at a window and appeared almost immediately.

"You'll stay with us," Brother James Connelly said. "There won't be a hotel room within 100 kilometers." Mbasa Kilu fetched Mr. Raymond Perotta's bags and took him to the guest room in the brothers' house.

Mr. Raymond Perotta attended the rest of the practice that afternoon, plus practices on Friday and Saturday, sometimes watching the play, mostly chatting with his friend Brother James Connelly.

During a break in practice on Saturday, the team was gathered around the ice water when one of the players said, "Give it a ride, Mbasa Kilu!" Knowing Mr. Raymond Perotta was in the stands, Mbasa Kilu was embarrassed. He tried to wave off the request. That only got others started. "Go for it, Mbasa Kilu!" they shouted. "Give it a ride!" Now even one of the older players called out. "See how far up you can put it," he said. Mbasa Kilu looked to Tedu Ngraeba for help. "It's okay," Tedu Ngraeba said. "Go ahead and kick it."

Without walking onto the field, Mbasa Kilu picked up one of the practice balls, took a wobbly step, and with a quick snap of his leg sent it high into the great oak tree. The ball picked its way through the branches and struck the main trunk four meters from the top, then started its long descent back to earth, striking every branch on the way. The team erupted into applause for Mbasa Kilu and were still pointing *Good Health!* to him when Coach Luke Omayinka ordered practice to resume. The break seemed to leave the entire team relaxed and confident as they clicked through the remaining drills. The mood persisted through the championship win on Sunday afternoon.

For the second straight year, Douglastown methodically put away a helpless Sherbourne City team for the championship. Douglastown dominated in all respects but the score, which was kept close by several pathetic calls by the referees, in two instances awarding successful penalty kicks to Sherbourne City, who still were unable to prevail. Mr. Raymond Perotta and Brother James Connelly — even though they both came from the U.S. — were good fans of Douglastown football, and watched the game with interest. They also made plans for getting Mr. Raymond Perotta back to the airport the next day. It was decided that the next morning Mbasa Kilu would drive Mr. Raymond Perotta to Brightwood Crossing, where a shuttle would take him the rest of the way to the airport.

Monday morning Mbasa Kilu gassed up the brothers' car and picked up Mr. Raymond Perotta and his luggage from the brothers' house. Mr. Raymond Perotta and Brother James Connelly shook hands on the porch. "Till next year," said Mr. Raymond Perotta. "Next year," answered Brother James Connelly.

* * * * *

Mbasa Kilu and Mr. Raymond Perotta rode a few minutes in silence until Mr. Raymond Perotta spoke. "Where did you learn to kick like that?" he asked. When Mbasa Kilu looked confused, he added, "Kicking it that high into the tree?"

Mbasa Kilu didn't know what to answer. Could not Mr. Raymond Perotta see his feet turned in and his ankles bent, which many said was a sign that the Great Spirit had punished him from birth? But it was the feet turned in and the ankles bent that caused him to kick this way, to kick the ball into the great tree, instead of into the goal, to kick the ball in a way that it would not score a goal — no matter how high it went.

"You must have practiced a lot," said Mr. Raymond Perotta.

Mbasa Kilu thought of Tedu Ngraeba's encouragement. He thought of the teammates who cried out, "Give it a ride, Mbasa Kilu. Give it a ride." But he thought this would sound silly to Mr. Raymond Perotta, so he did not mention it.

He also thought about the jokes, the jokes about the Air Force and unguided missiles. But he did not mention this, either.

"I don't know," he answered. "I practiced some, I guess," he said, not knowing what Mr. Raymond Perotta thought.

Mbasa Kilu was relieved to deliver Mr. Raymond Perotta to the airport shuttle in Brightwood Crossing and be on his way home, and be finished with trying to answer troubling questions.

* * * * *

The day after the championship game, the *Douglastown Draft* mentioned the presence of renowned NFL scout Mr. Raymond Perotta at the game. But the appearance of Mr. Raymond Perotta was soon forgotten as the season ended.

It was certainly forgotten as evil events began to transpire. But is it time yet for the story of evil events? Not yet. More details in the lives of Tedu Ngraeba and Mbasa Kilu must be told first.

* * * * *

Mbasa Kilu was still Mission Caretaker since turning down the offer of the Archbishop to go to the Big Doctor in Indoniva to undergo the surgery said to heal the feet turned in and the ankles bent.

Even though he was still Mission Caretaker, and not a mid-fielder himself, and would not write his memoirs and would not be interviewed by Ofi Leiya or be the subject of a miniseries for Provincial TV, Mbasa Kilu played an important role. First, he was selected by Tedu Ngraeba himself to be Team Manager. Not team mascot — Team Manager, whose job was to gather the equipment and load it onto the team bus before the game, and load the ball bag onto the team bus, and make sure the jerseys from the previous game were laundered and distributed to the players, and purchase the ice and have on hand the cold drink during the game, and see that none of the extra balls from the ball bag were allowed to roll onto the field during the game, and after the game clean the mud from the cleats and provide the towels and load the extra balls once again into the ball bag and onto the bus, and equipment onto the bus, and jerseys back into the laundry, and so on and so on, many other duties not able to be named. And Mbasa Kilu did the many duties in the same way he did the job of Mission Caretaker, with care and attention and diligence and without error.

And although Mbasa Kilu was careful never to allow any of the extra balls onto the field during a real game he nevertheless continued his practice of kicking on the sidelines, kicking an extra ball into the great oak tree. And Tedu Ngraeba still encouraged him and other players, too, encouraged him and shouted, "Give it a ride, Mbasa Kilu!" and "Atta boy, Mbasa Kilu!" and so on. And of course there was, behind the back of Tedu Ngraeba, still the occasional gesture of *Not-Right-in-the-Head*, sometimes even from the same players who shouted "Give it a ride, Mbasa Kilu!" Though in general the players on the Douglastown Leopards, some of them veteran players, long since out of high school, some of them with wives and children, were encouraging to Mbasa Kilu, and appreciated his work and his diligence and his care and his never making an error, and did not use the gesture of *Not-Right-in-the-Head*!

Now and then one of the players would see Mbasa Kilu kicking the extra ball on the sidelines, high into the great oak tree, he would take it upon himself to give Mbasa Kilu tips on lowering the trajectory of his kicks so that perhaps, one day, with practice, Mbasa Kilu would be able to kick the game ball low along the ground and into the net for a goal. (Though how Mbasa Kilu, with his feet turned in and his ankles bent and his wobbly step, was to run up and down the field and keep up with the other players and play a position — how this was to happen they were never able to explain.) And Mbasa Kilu would try obligingly to follow the tips and advice given, but each time it was the same, and he would kick the ball higher, much higher, than any goal would permit, or else dribble it pathetically along the ground so that yes, it was low enough, but without any fire, and before it reached the goal every defenseman in the league, in fact every schoolboy at the White Franciscan Sisters' School, would have blocked it or swept it to the side. And soon the giver of instruction, the giver of tips and advice, would abandon the project of teaching Mbasa Kilu a more suitable kick. And soon Mbasa Kilu would go to see about the equipment, or fuss with the ice and the cold drink, or gather up the additional balls and place them in the ball bag, or would line up the additional balls side by side along the fence at the edge of the practice field, or simply would be back to kicking the extra ball high into the great oak tree. And the giver of instruction, the giver of tips and advice, would turn away frustrated, and someone else would pick up from there by shouting, "Give it a ride, Mbasa Kilu!" or "Atta Boy, Mbasa Kilu!" and so on.

Mbasa Kilu's life extended beyond his duties as Team Manager of the Douglastown Leopards. For football was only one day a week for the game, and practice four or five evenings per week, for three hours or so, and then only four months of the year. So what of the other hours in Mbasa Kilu's day? What of the other days in his week? What of the other months in his year?

First of all, as we have said, Mission Caretaker, a demanding job, with many things to be looked after, many duties to perform, many requests of Brother Jerome Jenkins to be met, not to mention directions given by Miss Rose, the Mission Housekeeper, not to mention taking care to see that the great doors of the Annex were raised each morning so that the ladies were able to do their work, produce their brightly colored rugs to be sold in the market, sew their stylish dresses, much in the same fashion as those worn by Sister Sheila McMurphy. Not to mention: *Additional Duties.*

Additional duties were given him by Brother Jerome Jenkins, when it was clear that Mbasa Kilu was able to handle the work of Mission Caretaker carefully and efficiently and without error. For example, Brother Jerome Jenkins had Mbasa Kilu plant a garden right there in the Mission compound, to grow strange vegetables like asparagus and rhubarb and broccoli, imported from Brother Jerome Jenkins's brother-in-law in the U.S.

Another example, nailing up the frame and the chicken wire outside the Annex Building, to form the Day Care Area. And Mbasa Kilu was proud of the additional duties.

But to speak of *Day Care Area?* Here we are getting ahead of the story. We haven't yet said why day care was needed, or who needed it. Even though this is the story of Mbasa Kilu, the Mission Caretaker, much of it relates nevertheless to Tedu Ngraeba and Ofi Leiya. And the story of Day Care Area goes back to the Archbishop's visit, when Mbasa Kilu spoke privately to Ofi Leiya, and asked her, was there someone else? And asked her, is it Tedu Ngraeba? And Ofi Leiya answered yes to both questions. Because truly Ofi Leiya loved Tedu Ngraeba, and Tedu Ngraeba truly loved Ofi Leiya, and each was truly devoted to the other, and each of them, Tedu Ngraeba and Ofi Leiya, had eyes only for each other.

So, first you need to hear the story of Ofi Leiya and Tedu Ngraeba, the story of truly devoted, the story of eyes only for each other. And also that Tedu Ngraeba was working successfully as a member of the construction crew building the dual roadway through the Maryville Region connecting Douglastown and Brightwood Crossing, eventually going all the way to Harbourtown. And after only six months, Tedu Ngraeba was appointed Crew Chief and was given responsibility for twelve other men and was given to drive the crew truck to and from the work site and the big Regional Garage, formerly the Imperial Air Force Hangar, on the outskirts of Douglastown.

Crew Chief. That was the downfall. There will be more to the story of Crew Chief.

* * * * *

So, my friends, you have heard the first part of fame — the part having to do with football and career; the part having to do with championships, with running through the opposition, with making last minute goals; the part having to do with being a good worker, with being promoted to Crew Chief.

Then there was the part of fame having to do with being a father. Because the week after graduation Tedu Ngraeba and Ofi Leiya were married. And the next year — just after the first of Tedu Ngraeba's promising football seasons, but before the first championship — they had their first child. It was a boy.

The newspapers who one week ran front page photos of the winning goal the next week ran photos of the proud father and beautiful mother and their new son, Martin.

There were photos of the happy couple leaving the hospital, Tedu Ngraeba pushing his wife in a wheelchair, while she held their new son, Martin. There were photos of the happy family arriving at their home in Orchid Gardens, driven by Ofi Leiya's brother Thomas.

Women looking at the photos of the baby said, *He looks like his father.* Men said, *He looks like a midfielder.*

Mbasa Kilu looked at the photos and said *His mother is beautiful.* Then, not wanting to seem to be jealous, Mbasa Kilu said, *They are my two best friends.* Then he added, looking at Martin, *The baby also. They are my three best friends.*

Two Sundays later the baby was baptized. There were more photos. The happy couple arriving at St. Peter Claver Church. The crowd of relatives gathered around the baptismal font, all eyes on the baby. The baby just starting to cry as the first drops of water touched his forehead. Father Julius Tsungula making a cross on the baby's forehead with the holy oil. The happy couple leaving St. Peter Claver Church, relatives showering them with rose petals.

During all this Mbasa Kilu stood in the background and beamed. Mbasa Kilu, the Mission Caretaker, had cleaned and prepared the church especially for this occasion, had scrubbed the baptismal font, had shined the brass lid which covered the baptismal font during the week. Mbasa Kilu could tell that Tedu Ngraeba noticed this special cleaning and shining as he entered the church: he pointed *Good Health!* to Mbasa Kilu over the heads of the relatives surrounding him.

* * * * *

Tedu Ngraeba was chosen to be Crew Chief, not because he was known by all in the region as the top football player: he was chosen because he was fair, because he worked hard himself, because he inspired those who worked for him to do their best.

And right about the time he was elevated to Crew Chief, a memo came down from the regional office in Brightwood Crossing. The memo told of a collection that would benefit all workers because it was for The Party (which was in effect the government). The collection was voluntary, said the memo. Anyone who wanted to benefit The Party (that is, the government) could contribute. It would not *have* to be 10 percent of salary, said the memo, but whatever the worker could afford, for The Party, for the benefit of everyone. When the memo came down, Tedu Ngraeba thought of the fat Party bosses and fat government bosses in Brightwood Crossing, filling each others' pockets. "They are not interested in the benefit of everyone," he said. "They are interested only in the benefit of themselves." But Tedu Ngraeba knew he was responsible to Brightwood Crossing, so he posted the memo on the bulletin board at regional work headquarters. "Let everyone decide what he wants to give," he said to himself.

* * * * *

Tedu Ngraeba was made Crew Chief because he was a leader, because he was fair. If he said to one person, do this, and to another, do that — he was fair, giving them jobs suited to them, giving them jobs of equal effort and stress. If he saw a person reporting late in the morning, and he called the person aside and said, *This must stop,* you knew he was being fair. You knew he didn't say it after the first, even after the second time. You knew if he said it the person had gotten in the *habit* of late sleep, probably late flask at night and late sleep in the morning. You knew it was a habit gone far enough, that something had to stop, that the correction was fair, because Tedu Ngraeba was fair. And wasn't this the same as he had acted in his youth as captain of the football team, the district champion football team, at Maryville Regional Vocational High School? Yes. And hadn't he received the Brother Josephus medal for outstanding Leadership in Athletics and Academics? Yes.

So when Tedu Ngraeba took Marvin Kindola aside (even though Marvin was his own cousin) and told him, *This must stop,* you knew he was being fair. And if you worked for Tedu Ngraeba, you knew that Marvin Kindola not only had come late but had missed the truck the day before, staying out of work the entire day. You knew it had become a *habit*. You knew it was time for Tedu Ngraeba to tell him, *This must stop.* And so he told Marvin Kindola, "This must stop." You knew that in saying that he was being fair.

Explain that to Marvin Kindola. The next week on Monday Marvin Kindola excused himself from work and went to the regional office and asked to speak to the Regional Supervisor. "I want to file a complaint," he said. The clerk said the Regional Supervisor was busy. She handed a form to Marvin Kindola and gestured toward a table with pencils where he could write it out.

But when he wrote it out, he did not write the words *Tedu Ngraeba said this must stop,* or the words *Tedu Ngraeba made an unfair correction,* or the words *Tedu Ngraeba is unfair.* He wrote, "Tedu Ngraeba did not properly pass the word for Party contributions." This was Marvin Kindola, who had been late more than once. This was Marvin Kindola, who had missed the truck to the work site and kept himself out of work for the day. This was Marvin Kindola, who himself had not given a Party contribution.

"Will I hear?" Marvin Kindola asked the clerk when he gave her the form. She shrugged, dropping the form into a tray of other forms and letters. "Sometimes it takes a while," she said.

* * * * *

Marvin Kindola, after that day, stopped coming late to work. He did not stop the late flasks at night. Nor was he the most diligent worker on the work crew. But he never again missed the truck to the work site. Whoever thought about it, thought Tedu Ngraeba had done the right thing to tell him, *This must stop.* They thought that would be the end of it. And for then, it *was* the end of it.

Under Tedu Ngraeba's leadership, the road crew got down to business. They stayed ahead of schedule. They did their job.

Then there was a strike of the hotel workers in the city, something to do with their medical care. In general, men on the work crew did not know the hotel workers, but Samuel Ghi had a girlfriend in the city who worked for the Empire Hotel, and she asked Samuel Ghi to enlist the support of the work crew. When Samuel Ghi brought the request to Tedu Ngraeba, Tedu Ngraeba thought about it carefully. He knew Samuel Ghi was a good worker. Tedu Ngraeba asked Ofi Leiya about the girlfriend. "A bright girl, a good girl," said Ofi Leiya. Tedu Ngraeba also knew the work crew was three days ahead of schedule. So he gave the men on the work crew permission to stage a four-hour strike in support of the hotel workers — "work stoppage," they called it; they didn't even call it a strike. Next morning, the work crew was back at work.

Eventually the strike of the hotel workers was settled. They did not get the health care they wanted, but the Party boss received assurances that it would be the first item brought up in the legislature the next session. Some said that the assurances were not all he got, that the settlement included a handsome payment to the Party boss from the hotel owners — a stipend, they called it — which he had to split with his representative in the legislature.

But the strike had been settled, and everyone thought that would be the end of it. And for then, it *was* the end of it.

* * * * *

So that is what the average person saw: a simple disagreement between the boss of the work crew and one of the workers, who mended his ways after being corrected; a mild demonstration of political activism on the part of a trade union — the hotel workers — ending in a settlement. You could say it was a slight stir, but ended peacefully. That is what appeared on the surface.

Behind the scenes, there was more. There was more to the interaction between Marvin Kindola and Tedu Ngraeba than the correction of Marvin Kindola's negligent work habits.

For a while it appeared the disagreement between Tedu Ngraeba and Marvin Kindola was settled. But one night after the work stoppage Marvin Kindola waited to speak to Tedu Ngraeba.

"I won big on the game last week," Marvin Kindola told him. Everyone knew that Marvin Kindola bet on the games. Everyone knew that betting on the games was illegal. Everyone knew that betting was permitted by the central government in exchange for stipends paid to key government officials by The Syndicate, which ran the on-line betting sites.

So it was no surprise to Tedu Ngraeba to hear of Marvin Kindola's betting activity. "What you do away from work is of no concern to me," Tedu Ngraeba said. "What you do with your money is not my business."

"Fair enough," said Marvin Kindola. He acknowledged that as a player Tedu Ngraeba was right not to be betting. "You can only play to win," he said. "But," he said, "there is no reason why we can't both win."

Ofi Leiya said later that Tedu Ngraeba found Marvin Kindola to be what he called a "tiresome" person. He always had some far-fetched notion of how he would get rich — without, of course, having to work for it. Tedu Ngraeba would take the time to listen only because he could usually punch holes in the scheme. And he didn't want to appear to be afraid of Marvin Kindola's outlandish ideas. And Marvin Kindola being his cousin, he felt a family responsibility to keep him out of trouble — a hope that over the years had turned to despair.

This time the scheme involved betting — Marvin Kindola's betting, of course. Douglastown had risen to such daunting superiority over their lesser opponents that it was not surprising for the betting sites to make them three- and even four-goal favorites. In such instances, Marvin Kindola's scheme was this: he would bet in anticipation of a Douglastown win, but at a margin less than the betting spread. This way Tedu Ngraeba could still play to win. But in the closing minutes of play, Marvin Kindola explained, Tedu could relax the team's defenses so that their opponent could score and edge closer than expected, closer than the spread allowed.

The only thing that surprised Tedu Ngraeba about the scheme was that for the first time Marvin Kindola proposed something not only ill-advised but illegal. Not only illegal in the eyes of the Central Government and the police, but at cross purposes with the interests of The Syndicate, who controlled the organization *ClereBet,* which ran the betting sites. If word got out that games were being fixed, the integrity of the betting sites would be destroyed. Bettors would take their money elsewhere. The Central Government and the police would be indifferent, but if The Syndicate heard that Marvin Kindola was making the betting sites his own private profit center — at their expense — there would be hell to pay.

"First of all," Tedu Ngraeba said, "you know I would never consent to such a scheme. But I should warn you, you don't want to mess with The Syndicate." Tedu Ngraeba could have let it go at that, but he put his better judgment aside. He chided Marvin Kindola with one more thing. "I thought you would know better," he said.

At that point Marvin Kindola made *his* biggest mistake. Perhaps he was stung by the dismissive refusal. Perhaps he actually thought he was in a position of advantage. But he laid down a gauntlet for Tedu Ngraeba. "I thought *you* would know better," he snapped back, "than to promote a labor strike in support of the Hotel Workers. I would hate for this to get back to The Syndicate. You know they own The Regal Hotel in Brightwood Crossing."

Ofi Leiya said Tedu Ngraeba considered this more humorous than threatening, since The Syndicate had controlled every aspect of the Hotel Workers' settlement, and had done so without doing anything to quash the strike, giving them a mantle of labor fairness.

"Nevertheless," she said later, "there was nothing he could really do. He wasn't about to accept money from Marvin Kindola. Reporting him to the police or the Central Government would do no good. And he had no contact with The Syndicate, and wanted nothing to do with them." She said she begged him to tell Marvin Kindola that he was letting the matter drop. But she knew Tedu Ngraeba was not about to do that, either.

He could have told Coach Luke Omayinka, thought Mbasa Kilu. This was the same suggestion Ofi Leiya had made to him. But Tedu Ngraeba was afraid of causing a reaction, afraid the coach would go to the police, or afraid Coach Luke Omayinka would withdraw him from the lineup. So Tedu Ngraeba insisted on bearing the entire responsibility on his own shoulders. Not knowing, of course, what would follow.

What followed not long after took everyone by surprise.

* * * * *

It was only after the Douglastown Leopards had completed the regular season and entered the playoffs that trouble started. There is no agreement on what the first sign of trouble was. Was it when the first arrest occurred? A Military Police van with government soldiers showed up, not on the road to Maryville, not during the work day, but later in the evening, outside the Douglastown Leopards practice field. They had a paper for the arrest of Alvin Johnson.

Alvin Johnson also worked for the road crew. Earlier in the year, he had participated in the work stoppage in support of the hotel workers. But so had Tedu Ngraeba. So had the rest of the team — except of course those few who had jobs elsewhere — like Thomas Smith, who worked in his father's repair shop in Douglastown, and the handful who worked in the quarry.

When Tedu Ngraeba attempted to talk to the Military Police sergeant in charge — he was given the cold shoulder. "We've got our orders," said the sergeant, holding out a green carbon of the arrest warrant. "Read for yourself."

Tedu Ngraeba took the copy. Under *Charge,* it read *Theft.* That was all it said: *Theft.*

When the Military Police van had left, other members of the team who were also members of the road crew spoke up. Earlier in the year, they said, Alvin Johnson had found a hub cap in the grass by the side of the road. He kept it, took it to Maryville next time he went, and sold it in the market. The hub cap dealer was notorious, they said, for accepting stolen property and reselling it — even though Alvin Johnson had *found* the hub cap, not stolen it.

Tedu Ngraeba nodded, but he still wanted to know why. *Theft* was the excuse, not the why. But what was the why, and what was to be done about it?

Before Tedu Ngraeba could figure out the why, before he could figure out what was to be done about it, the soldiers appeared again, this time in a stake truck marked with the Military Police insignia, this time in the middle of the working day. A burly sergeant stepped down from the cab with papers. Eight other soldiers with rifles dropped down from the back of the truck and stood behind him. Despite the heat they were dressed in helmets and full fatigues. The sergeant seemed to know whom he wanted. Ignoring Tedu Ngraeba, he went directly to three of the work crew and tapped them on the chest. "You are under arrest," he said, and the soldiers with rifles forced them to climb into the back of the truck.

This time the green carbon simply said *charges.*

Tedu Ngraeba stepped forward after reading the paper. "Charges?" he said. "What are the charges?"

The burly sergeant gave him a blank look. "They will be told," he said, and brushed by Tedu Ngraeba and climbed back into the cab.

When the soldiers left this time, no one came forward. There was no *theft* to explain the arrests of the three. There was no hub cap, lost or stolen.

If the work stoppage was a problem, if the work stoppage was even known about, none of them — or Alvin Johnson before them — were what you would call leaders of the work stoppage. All were members of the work crew. All were part of the starting eleven of Douglastown.

When the work crew returned to the garage that evening, Tedu Ngraeba got hold of town solicitor Jeremy Ogangwu. Jeremy was four years out of law school, and since the retirement of his father, Jonathan Ogangwu, he sold marriage licenses from his little store-front office on Main Road. Every three months when the district magistrate came to town, he helped prepare and present cases brought by the citizens of Douglastown.

After discussing it with Jeremy Ogangwu and after the two of them together talked to the elder, Jonathan Ogangwu, it was decided Tedu Ngraeba and Jeremy would drive to Brightwood Crossing and get a hearing, try to get the men released, or at least find out what was required.

At the police station, a lone soldier with an AK-47 stood outside the Police Captain's office — not a policeman, but a Royal Guard soldier. Jeremy Ogangwu was greeted by officers and secretaries who knew him from his duties as a solicitor. Several evidently knew Tedu Ngraeba as well — his football exploits by then having spread nationwide. A friendly receptionist promised Jeremy Ogangwu and Tedu Ngraeba a meeting with the Police Captain. In fact the Captain came into the outer office long enough to shake hands with them and compliment Tedu Ngraeba on Douglastown's recent win. "But you better be careful," he said. "Mount Elliott is coming back strong this year." Mount Elliott was to be Douglastown's next playoff opponent.

"I know why you're here," he told Jeremy Ogangwu. "I'll be with you as soon as I've got a minute." The Captain disappeared back into his office.

An hour passed. Another hour. Almost three hours later, a clerk emerged from one of the offices with a clipboard. She was deferential and apologetic to Jeremy Ogangwu. "The captain is gone for the day," she said. "He sent his regrets. He asked that I help you."

She had the same green carbon copy of the arrest form the sergeant had presented to Tedu Ngraeba when Alvin Johnson had been arrested and showed it to Jeremy Ogangwu. Looking over Jeremy Ogangwu's shoulder, Tedu Ngraeba recognized the charge at the bottom: *Theft.*

"How about the others?" asked Jeremy Ogangwu. "They will be charged separately," said the clerk. But the hearing had not yet been conducted. No, they could not be seen, said the clerk. Only if they select a solicitor. They had been given the opportunity, said the clerk. Behind her the Royal Guard soldier shifted his position.

"I can help you fill out an *Offer to Represent* form," said the clerk. "It's offering your services," she said. "If they accept, you can speak with them."

Jeremy Ogangwu breathed hard but agreed to fill out the form. The clerk remained gracious, but insisted on filling out the information herself. She gave up the form only for Jeremy Ogangwu to sign and Tedu Ngraeba to sign as a witness.

"A person has got to learn to hold his tongue," Jeremy Ogangwu said to Tedu Ngraeba after they were back on the street.

That Saturday a supposedly reinvigorated Mount Elliott team showed up for the playoff game. But they were not the Mount Elliott of old. Although the Douglastown team of Tedu Ngraeba, Wing Omo, five other regulars, and four substitute players made several mistakes on defense, they eventually prevailed, 4-3. The winning goal came when Tedu Ngraeba, triple-teamed in the right corner, was able to center the ball to Wing Omo in front of the net, who punched it past a helpless Mount Elliott keeper.

Need we mention it was the last assist by Tedu Ngraeba in his young career? Need we mention it was the last victory by Douglastown in the Tedu Ngraeba era? They advanced to the semi-final against Harbourtown, but it was a match that would never be held.

Except for the usual handshakes, there was little celebration after the game. Before the crowd had cleared the stadium and the nearby fields, Tedu Ngraeba was headed to the Main Road office of Jeremy Ogangwu to plot the strategy for the coming week.

The last memory anyone had of Tedu Ngraeba alive was the next morning, leaving the compound in the black jeep, once again driving himself and Jeremy Ogangwu to Brightwood Crossing.

Later that afternoon, Brother Jerome Jenkins took the call from the district police. The brothers' black jeep had been involved in a single car accident. The car had run off the road into a giant tree. Tedu Ngraeba was killed. Jeremy Ogangwu was in critical condition with a fractured skull and multiple internal injuries.

By the time Mbasa Kilu and Brother Jerome Jenkins arrived at the hospital, Ofi Leiya and her friends from the sewing group were already there, informed by a cell phone call from one of the nurses.

Ofi Leiya was holding Martin and weeping uncontrollably. Her girl friends from the sewing group and several of the nurses she knew surrounded her — themselves weeping aloud.

Some offered to take Martin from Ofi Leiya, but she held on the tighter, too distraught to let go of him.

Brother Jerome Jenkins visited briefly with Jeremy Ogangwu, but he was too injured to talk sense, seemed to remember nothing of the accident, seemed unaware that there *was* an accident.

Since Ofi Leiya was unable, Brother Jerome Jenkins made arrangements for claiming Tedu Ngraeba's body and bringing it back to Douglastown for burial. From there he would arrange the funeral with Father Victor Woluska.

On the drive back to Douglastown they stopped at the bridge where the accident occurred. The car had been removed, but there was still broken glass in the grass on the side of the road and around the giant tree; the tree had a big bare spot where bark had been ripped off by the collision. Brother Jerome Jenkins stayed at the scene for several minutes, stepping off the distance from the road to the tree. Mbasa Kilu saw that there were no skid marks in the grass. "Tedu Ngraeba was a good driver," he thought. "Why would Tedu Ngraeba not put on his brakes?" he thought. He and Brother Jerome Jenkins looked at one another but said nothing on the remaining trip back to Douglastown.

* * * * *

Hundreds attended the funeral — held in St. Peter Claver church. Shining up the church for the funeral, Mbasa Kilu thought of Martin's baptism day. The task he performed was the same as then, but this time it was without the joy of the baptism day. This time it was done with sadness; sadness that Martin was without a father; sadness that Ofi Leiya had lost her husband; sadness that Mbasa Kilu had lost a friend; sadness that the world had lost a good man.

Dressed in their black and gold football silks and black stockings, the team bore the coffin and lined the aisle. Martin, confused by the ceremony, smiled at familiar members of the team as he walked in holding his mother's hand. Ofi Leiya — her eyes down, by now exhausted of tears — looked neither right nor left. Her sister walked beside her. Behind them were various aunts and uncles, the Mayor of Douglastown in his suit and tie and blue sash, the Mount Elliott coach and the great Jimbo Akaya and several others who Mbasa Kilu recognized as members of the Mount Elliott team, six of the White Franciscan

Sisters, several of whom Mbasa Kilu recognized as teachers from St. Peter Claver elementary school.

Only at the end of the funeral Mass, when the crowds inside the church spilled into the courtyard outside, did Mbasa Kilu notice the hundreds lining the road to the cemetery. Only then did he notice the soldiers spaced every 20 meters along the same route.

For over a half hour the procession crawled its way to the cemetery. At the gravesite Father Victor Woluska attempted a few words. "Lord," he said, "Lord, help us in our sorrow." But he could get no farther. Ofi Leiya collapsed beside the grave. Her sister took Martin, who began to cry. Wing Omo and two members of the team gently helped Ofi Leiya into a chair. Father Victor hurriedly murmured the committal prayers, raising his voice at the end. "Amen," he said. "Amen," echoed the crowd, still strung along the road and out the front gate of the cemetery.

What a young life!

Mbasa Kilu remained behind with the gravediggers, helping them fill in the grave. He didn't even think about the next day, or the next moment.

Section 3 — The Scout

The week of Tedu Ngraeba's funeral the Douglastown Leopards forfeited their playoff game, putting a mediocre Harbourtown team in the finals. Then Harbourtown surprised everyone by prevailing against Oil City for the championship.

Coach Luke Omayinka held a final meeting of the Douglastown Leopards on Monday to collect uniforms and formally end the season. But instead of an exhortation toward the following year, he delivered a eulogy for the team that was. "You were a great team," he told them. "Who could have known it would come to this?" The season was over. Football was over. It seemed as if life were over.

The following Monday, Alvin Johnson and his three teammates were taken before the magistrate, who dismissed the charges, setting the four of them free, to ride the afternoon bus back to Douglastown.

Mbasa Kilu laundered the uniforms one last time and stored them with the equipment in the garage. The rest of the summer he performed his duties as Mission Caretaker with no enthusiasm, wondering what the Fall would bring. Wing Omo became Crew Chief on the road project, which was creeping its way toward Brightwood Crossing. Each morning the crew truck would pull out in a cloud of dust, but without the usual banter.

Marvin Kindola got a job in the oil fields, making twice the salary of a road crew worker, and moved to his own apartment in Oil City. In less than two months, he became an assistant vice president of the oil workers' union. The basic purpose of the union was to collect dues to be split between the officers of the union and the government officials assigned to oversee them. And now there were members of the military who insisted on their cut.

In return for paying their dues, union members were allowed to keep their jobs another year.

Someone said Marvin Kindola's uncle knew an official in the government who had arranged the union job. Mbasa Kilu didn't know who had arranged it. *Good riddance,* he thought. People knew of the differences Marvin Kindola had with Tedu Ngraeba, but no one connected him with Tedu Ngraeba's death. At least no one spoke of it out loud. Mbasa Kilu wondered about this, but kept it to himself.

* * * * *

It didn't take long for Mbasa Kilu to find out what the Fall would bring: it would bring the same thing it brought every year, but without Tedu Ngraeba.

Without fanfare or election or appointment, Wing Omo became captain of the Douglastown team. Perhaps it took place privately, with Coach Luke Omayinka, about the same time Wing Omo became Crew Chief.

Mbasa Kilu's own job as team manager began again officially when the Mission Housekeeper complained that football equipment was blocking her path to the yams. And anyway wasn't it time for the season to start again and all that stuff to be removed from the garage, and out of her way? Unless Mbasa Kilu thought *he* would like to be the person to fetch all the food and cook for 12 people every night, and crawl over a pile of football equipment in the process?

Mbasa Kilu moved the extra equipment to the shed beside the practice pitch, and took advantage of having five extra practice balls to practice kicking at the great oak tree. The ball felt good striking the inside of his left foot. It made him feel closer to Tedu Ngraeba. *Give it a ride, Mbasa Kilu,* he could hear in his memory. For Mbasa Kilu, kicking the ball at the great oak tree became not only a physical release but a sort of meditation.

Meanwhile the team muddled along without Tedu Ngraeba. They devoted a moment of silence to Tedu Ngraeba at their opening game. After that he was absent without comment.

Wing Omo was a capable leader, though he would not achieve the levels set by Tedu Ngraeba. Nevertheless, the team won 10 of their first 16 matches and qualified for the playoffs. Moreover, they were gaining momentum as they approached their first playoff match.

Mbasa Kilu had prepared the equipment for the match (which would be at home) and was taking his accustomed practice kicks at the great oak tree when a red checkered cab from Sherbourne City pulled into the compound and discharged its passenger in front of the brothers' house.

Mbasa Kilu recognized Mr. Raymond Perotta and immediately wondered, *Has anyone told him about Tedu Ngraeba?*

Brother James Connelly came out on the porch to meet him, and Mbasa Kilu was about to go and fetch Mr. Raymond Perotta's luggage, when the two men disappeared into the house and the cab driver fetched the bag in as well — and then drove off.

Mbasa Kilu returned to his kicking, then knocked off when the Mission Housekeeper called him to carry a bushel from the garden into the kitchen for her.

Mr. Raymond Perotta did not appear at dinner that night with the brothers and Mbasa Kilu. Brother James Connelly was busy talking at the table with Brother Jogues about what it would cost to replace the old accounting books at the high school and whether a new and different book was not a better idea. Nobody talked about why Mr. Raymond Perotta was there. Next morning, however, when Mbasa Kilu emerged from his one-room apartment at the rear of the Annex to head for the practice field, he saw Mr. Raymond Perotta on the porch of the brothers' house, drinking his morning coffee.

It was Saturday, so the ladies would not be working. The huge garage doors did not have to be opened, the huge fans would not be turned on. There was only the game to be prepared for — the first playoff game. Fetch the practice equipment from the shed; lay out the uniforms and towels in the locker room; too early yet, but eventually, purchase the ice and chip it; and have the cold drink on hand before the start of the match.

Mbasa Kilu was surprised when Mr. Raymond Perotta appeared beside him. "I was sorry when I heard about your friend," he said to Mbasa Kilu. He said Brother James Connelly had notified him in the states. "Everybody talks about what a great person he was," said Mr. Raymond Perotta. "And what a midfielder!"

They were silent for a moment. Mbasa Kilu felt awkward discussing Tedu Ngraeba. He thought of the evil events, but didn't mention them.

"And how's the kicking going?" Mr. Raymond Perotta asked Mbasa Kilu. Mbasa Kilu remembered the drive to the airport the last time Mr. Raymond Perotta was there, and he was embarrassed again. "It's okay," he answered.

Mbasa Kilu explained that he had to be heading for the practice field to prepare for the game. "That's all right," Mr. Raymond Perotta said, "I'll walk along." While Mbasa Kilu did his work, Mr. Raymond Perotta was full of questions about the game, the season, the team. This was familiar territory for Mbasa Kilu. Unlike talking about himself or Tedu Ngraeba, he felt more comfortable answering Mr. Raymond Perotta's questions about football, when necessary providing statistical backup for his answers.

Could the team make the finals without Tedu Ngraeba? "Maybe," said Mbasa Kilu. He explained that the team wasn't the same without Tedu Ngraeba, but that more and more every week the team was coming together around Wing Omo. They won only half their first ten matches, but since then won five out of six.

"I guess at the end of today we'll begin to know the answer," said Mr. Raymond Perotta.

"One more thing," said Mr. Raymond Perotta. "I saw you practicing your kicks yesterday when I arrived," he said. "I know you're busy with the playoffs starting," he said, "but maybe we could get together Monday or Tuesday."

Mbasa Kilu was surprised. He wanted to say, *Get together for what?* "Where?" he blurted instead.

"Can we meet right here?" Mr. Raymond Perotta said. "On the sideline. Maybe an hour before practice starts, on Monday. And we can just use the practice balls, if that's okay?"

"Okay," said Mbasa Kilu. But it wasn't really okay: his mind was spinning. Long before this Mbasa Kilu had determined he would never play real football, with his feet turned in and his ankles bent. What was Mr. Raymond Perotta's idea? Didn't he realize that the kicks would never score a goal? Was he trying to be nice? Or was this just another of the many odd elements of U.S. football?

It was like that the rest of the day, throughout the match, in which Douglastown defeated Port Osmond to advance to the second round — as expected, but only by a goal, not the margin expected. Twice Wing Omo had broken away for clear shots at the goal, only to be tripped up from behind by a Port Osmond player. Both times the referee ruled it incidental contact. The referees didn't seem to mind that this was happening on the Douglastown home turf, with Douglastown fans screaming in disbelief after the second tripping incident was ignored.

Nevertheless, Douglastown advanced to round two of the playoffs, so the furor soon died out.

Mbasa Kilu was enough concerned with his own situation that he did not register the presence of Marvin Kindola in the crowd at the game.

Saturday night Mbasa Kilu tossed and turned, finally went to sleep, barely waking in time for Sunday Mass.

* * * * *

Brother James Connelly waited for him outside the church after Mass. "Mr. Perotta talked to me last night," he said. He tried to reassure Mbasa Kilu about the meeting with Mr. Perotta Monday before practice. "He is interested in your kicking," he said.

Mbasa Kilu had watched U.S. football with the brothers, who became emotionally involved in the game, shouting at each other and at the TV screen. To Mbasa Kilu it was a curious game, played by men wearing helmets and padding, who bashed their heads together when one of them made a good play. Now and then a player known as the kicker would come on the field briefly. If he was successful, the other players would smash their helmets into his. If he missed, they would ignore him and seat him alone on the sideline.

Even the idea of a special person for kicking was unheard of. Mbasa Kilu remembered Brother Mortimer Ygloso, the shop teacher, arguing about it with Brother James Connelly while they watched U.S. football on ESPN. "In true football, there is no kicker. We are *all* kickers," Brother Mortimer said. Which Brother James Connelly had to acknowledge was right, since five years before Jo Jo Chou, a forward, had been signed from the European Premier League to U.S. football for that very reason: to be a kicker.

Whatever the case, Mbasa Kilu kept it to himself, afraid that he himself would be the object of ridicule, along with U.S. football, if some members of the team found out that U.S. football was interested in him — whatever the reason.

* * * * *

Evenings, the road crew truck returned to Douglastown between four-thirty and five. Practice started at six. Monday Mbasa Kilu dabbled at his duties during the day before going to the practice pitch to prepare for practice. He had everything ready before four, before the road crew truck had even returned.

The venerable Coach Luke Omayinka wandered by the practice pitch during preparations, as he sometimes did. When was the last time the practice pitch had been rolled, he wanted to know. And if Douglastown advanced against Harbourtown, the defending champion, they would have to play at the Harbourtown pitch. When that happened, would Mbasa Kilu find out the dimensions of the Harbourtown pitch, and mark them off on the Douglastown practice pitch. Mbasa Kilu assured him he already had the dimensions of Harbourtown and Kittredge, and would mark them off the week before.

Before leaving, Coach Luke Omayinka looked him straight in the eye. "Good luck," he said. And he pointed *Good Health!* to him. Mbasa Kilu pointed *Good Health!* back. Then he had to turn away to keep from shedding a tear in front of him.

* * * * *

A few minutes before five Mr. Raymond Perotta appeared, trailing along with him two youngsters from the elementary school. He glanced at his watch, then at Mbasa Kilu. "Ready to go?" he asked. "Okay," said Mbasa Kilu.

Mr. Raymond Perotta gestured toward the pitch. "Why don't you just go out there and do your thing."

"Dexter and Logan will retrieve for us," he added, motioning the two boys to stand off the end of the pitch.

Mbasa Kilu had been up since before five, by now had rehearsed every possible scenario of this meeting. He picked up a couple of the practice balls, and felt awkward stumping out onto the practice pitch, taking his wobbly steps in front of Mr. Raymond Perotta. "You want me to kick, right?" he asked.

"Sure," said Mr. Raymond Perotta. "Just what you were doing," he said.

Mbasa Kilu looked at his tree in the corner, then at the goal at the end of the pitch. He knew he could not kick it *in* the goal, but he was afraid a kick into the tree might seem — well, childish. So instead he moved to a spot about 25 meters away from the goal and kicked a looping kick *toward* the goal — the ball landing 10 meters beyond the goal and rolling aimlessly off the grounds into a patch of bushes.

"Okay," said Mr. Raymond Perotta, "Good. Now how about the tree?" he said. "See how high you can get it."

This I know, thought Mbasa Kilu. With that he lifted a booming kick into the great oak tree beyond the corner of the field. Mr. Raymond Perotta said nothing as the ball bounced from limb to limb on the way down.

"Can you back up a bit?" Mr. Raymond Perotta said, tossing him another of the practice balls. So Mbasa Kilu moved back 10 meters or so and kicked again. The ball struck the great oak tree dead center in the top branches, once again bouncing from one limb to the other on the way to the ground as the boys scrambled to get it. Mbasa Kilu repeated the kick three more times, each time a little farther. Finally, when he was backed up nearly to the opposite end of the practice pitch, he kicked a ball which struck the great oak tree only halfway up from the ground. With this there was a noise behind him, and Mbasa Kilu noticed that several players had arrived early for practice and were quietly watching the proceedings from the stands.

"Okay, that's good," said Mr. Raymond Perotta. "Now, instead of the tree, how about right into the corner of the field."

Mbasa Kilu had never tried the corner of the pitch. His first kick veered off toward the center of the goal, crossing the end line and landing several meters beyond.

"Okay," said Mr. Raymond Perotta, "hit the corner if you can." But Mbasa Kilu's second and third and fourth kicks were the same.

With that a voice behind him called out. Mbasa Kilu turned to see that a dozen or so players had gathered for practice and were watching his kicking. Some were still in their work clothes; some had already changed into their practice shoes and shorts.

"Hit the can, Mbasa Kilu," called one of the players. There was a murmur of agreement from the others. Another called out, "Give it a ride, Mbasa Kilu. Hit the can."

Mr. Raymond Perotta looked toward the red trash can sitting off the sideline at the corner of the practice pitch. "The can. . .," he said. "Can you actually do that? Okay, hit the can."

Mbasa Kilu lofted a kick toward the sideline, the ball landing only a meter past the red can.

"Try it again," said Mr. Raymond Perotta. This time the ball landed square on target, dislodging the metal lid with a raucous clang. A cheer went up from the gallery behind him, followed by laughter and hand-slapping. Mr. Raymond Perotta looked on in amused disbelief as Mbasa Kilu lofted two more kicks within a meter or two of the can, followed by a third that knocked the can over, sending it rolling into the deeper grass.

By now more of the team had arrived for practice and were loudly cheering each kick. For them it was partly the affection they had developed for Mbasa Kilu. Partly it was a vindication of real football over U.S. football: here was Mbasa Kilu, prevented — by his feet turned in and his ankles bent — from even *playing* real football; in fact, some said, prevented from this by the Great Spirit; yet he was obviously impressing the scout from U.S. football.

Mr. Raymond Perotta had seen all he needed, and motioned the two ball retrievers to come in. He sought out the venerable coach Luke Omayinka waiting on the sideline, shook his hand, thanked him, and turned the pitch back over to him. Mbasa Kilu gathered the practice balls from the two youngsters before they departed with Mr. Raymond Perotta. "I'll get back to you," said Mr. Raymond Perotta to Mbasa Kilu, before walking off with the two boys.

* * * * *

The next day and the day after that, Mbasa Kilu performed his duties during the day before preparing for practice after work. Mr. Raymond Perotta did not speak with Mbasa Kilu, but Mbasa Kilu saw him spend an hour each afternoon on the brothers' porch, talking on his cell phone. The team's practices were sharp and spirited. The venerable coach Luke Omayinka kept the team focused on the upcoming playoff game, and after the excitement on the sidelines when Mbasa Kilu's kick hit the can, there was no further talk about Mr. Raymond Perotta and Mbasa Kilu and the kicking tryout, which is what Brother James Connelly called it. Above all, there wasn't the ridicule Mbasa Kilu feared.

Then, on the day of the last practice before the game, Brother James Connelly approached Mbasa Kilu as he was delivering a bushel of yams to the Mission Housekeeper.

She put up a hand. "Before he goes running off, he is to bring me a basket of rhubarb," she said. She continued about how she was trying to run a kitchen and if you want a meal cooked and rhubarb custard pie for Mr. Raymond Perotta's last meal with them she can't be in two places at once.

"*After* you help Miss Rose," said Brother James Connelly to Mbasa Kilu. "In the library."

Mbasa Kilu found Brother James Connelly and Mr. Raymond Perotta at the table in the library. Brother James Connelly did most of the talking. He explained that Mr. Perotta wanted Mbasa Kilu to come to the U.S. for a tryout. It would be after the playoffs were over.

Mbasa Kilu didn't know what to say. All he could think of was leaving the compound. "Who will do the chores?" he asked.

Brother James Connelly explained that Brother Jerome Jenkins already had help lined up. "And we can give you a ride to the airport," he said, anticipating Mbasa Kilu's next question. "Mbasa Kilu," he said, "you have a gift. It is worth giving it a try."

A Gift, thought Mbasa Kilu. He had never thought of it as a gift.

Mr. Raymond Perotta and Brother James Connelly urged him to take some time to think about it. Brother James

Connelly would phone Mr. Perotta back in the U.S. and let him know the decision.

* * * * *

The rest of the Douglastown season seemed to go by in a flash. That Saturday the team drove to Cooper Center, where they capitalized on sloppy play by the favored Coopers to bring home a two-goal victory, putting them in the finals the following week against Oil City.

On the bus ride to Oil City, the team bus was stopped twice at government checkpoints. Helmeted soldiers boarded the bus and slowly walked the aisle of the bus, shining flashlights into players' faces, going through some of their bags. Mbasa Kilu was forced to unpack the first aid kit, allowing a grim-faced soldier to paw through bandages and tubes of antibiotic salve. Another soldier stood outside beside the bus, pointing an AK-47 into the air.

When they finally arrived at the Oil City stadium, it was surrounded by soldiers holding AK-47s. In that part of the region there had been threats from rebel groups who had occasionally caused trouble.

The team was ushered into the visitors locker room, crowded with sacks of cement from a renovation project on the nearby sidewalks and courtyard.

In the Cooper Center victory, the officiating was improved over previous games; against Oil City, it sank to a new low. The teams played evenly, but whenever Douglastown mounted a drive, the referees managed to find a reason for stopping play. Oil City played aggressively, and their fouls were ignored, while three Douglastown players were given yellow cards for minor brushes. The result was that the team managed only one goal against Oil City's three. Douglastown missed out for the second year in a row. Oil City captured the title which had eluded them the year before.

Celebrating the Oil City victory was Marvin Kindola, now on his home turf.

This year, the second championship match after Tedu Ngraeba's death, Mbasa Kilu noticed that the newspaper columns and the sports blogs on the internet made no reference to the dominant Douglastown teams before the death of Tedu

Ngraeba. He had been buried in the press, just as he had been buried in the rain-filled grave just over a year before.

* * * * *

With the season now complete, Mbasa Kilu was able to turn his attention back to the question at hand. Hard as he tried to find a reason for *not* going to the U.S., everyone he talked to said he had but one choice: *Go.*

Brother Jerome Jenkins, who had unsuccessfully tried to get him to go with the Archbishop to be seen by the Big Doctor, now with renewed effort urged him to say yes to the offer of a tryout in the U.S. "What can you lose?" he asked. "It will be a great experience. And Mr. Raymond Perotta is an honest man."

Mbasa Kilu already knew Brother James Connelly was in favor. He continued to urge Mbasa Kilu to use the gift he had. "You will never again have such an opportunity," he said.

The venerable coach Luke Omayinka took the opportunity to pull Mbasa Kilu aside and register his opinion. "You've earned the right to try," he told Mbasa Kilu, "even if it comes to nothing."

Mbasa Kilu noticed that they spoke of the tryout as if it were an experience in itself — like a one-time visit to the Anthropology Museum at Brightwood Crossing. No one spoke as if the tryout might be successful, offering the possibility of a career in U.S. football.

Until Ofi Leiya talked to him. He knew Ofi Leiya would still be in mourning until the end of the year, and he had not spoken to her since her husband's death the year before. So he was surprised when a young girl from the elementary school tracked him down at work and said Ofi Leiya wished to talk to him. Surprised that she would want to talk with him. Frightened that he would say the wrong thing, that he would embarrass himself — as he had at the time of the Archbishop's visit.

Martin — now almost three — was playing outside when Mbasa Kilu visited. He ran inside to his mother when Mbasa Kilu turned in the front walk. Ofi Leiya was seated in a rocking chair in the small living room, wearing a white luyaà. She remained seated, but turned Martin around to greet him. "You remember your uncle," she told Martin. But he did not choose to remember, and simply buried his head in the folds of his mother's luyaà.

When she thanked Mbasa Kilu for preparing the church, he realized she was speaking of the funeral. He could only think of her collapsing by the grave, her sister taking Martin. Martin doesn't even *remember,* he realized.

"I heard of Mr. Raymond Perotta's visit," she said next. "He wants you to come to the U.S.?"

Mbasa Kilu nodded. He did not mention that Tedu Ngraeba's former teammates thought U.S. football was ridiculous, probably all the more ridiculous if Mbasa Kilu was going to play.

"How do you feel about it?" she asked.

Mbasa Kilu could do nothing but shrug. "I'm not sure," he said. What he realized was that he was not sure about making the trip to the U.S. It was not about U.S. football. It was about where he would eat; where he would stay; where he would sleep; how he would get back and forth to the practice pitch; what he would use for money. Mbasa Kilu felt too embarrassed to express these concerns, yet she seemed to read between the lines.

"Mbasa Kilu," she said, "nothing is sure. Nothing is certain. We can't see past the horizon — unless we keep walking."

"This is a wonderful opportunity," she said. "If Tedu were still here," she said, "he would urge you to go. You can still carry his spirit with you." She looked at him and reflected. "Tedu Ngraeba would be proud of you," she said. "He would want you to take the opportunity."

At that time he saw in Ofi Leiya's eyes that she meant it for his own good. Just as when she told him, "Speak from the heart." He could see in Ofi Leiya's eyes behind the sadness, behind the grief, that she believed he would use the opportunity. Not that she believed it was an opportunity for him to be a hero. Not that she believed he would play American football and leap in the air and score the winning goal. He could see in Ofi Leiya's eyes that she believed he would use the opportunity to make a good life. That he would use the opportunity to escape the sadness and bloodshed lurking in an uncertain future. That he would escape the grief of Tedu Ngraeba's death — something she could not yet do.

Book II

The U.S.

Section 4 — An Older Brother

So Mbasa Kilu *did* come to the U.S. for a tryout. This is how George Gardner came to know him. George Gardner was my father, and this is the story he told me.

My father was a quarterback for the New England Patriots in the late 2020s. He was pretty much a rolling stone during his playing career in the National Football League, before he was married and I was born. So when he asked if I would help him write about some of his experiences, I was glad to accept. I looked at it as a way to find out more about his life, which hadn't really interested me a lot when I was younger. And this would be a chance to spend more time with him.

You might imagine that my father was another of the outstanding New England quarterbacks at the beginning of the century — Drew Bledsoe, Tom Brady, Justin Byers. Not quite. A runner-up for the Heisman Trophy at Syracuse, George Gardner had three all-pro years at San Diego before signing a lucrative free agent contract with the Patriots. His first game with the Patriots he suffered a knee injury which put him out for the entire season. From there he struggled with knee injuries the remainder of his pro career, never lasting more than a few games, never fulfilling his promise.

As for my father's wish, it was less *his* story he wanted to tell as it was the story of Mbasa Kilu, whom my father felt had been almost forgotten by history, even though for years he has held the record for the longest field goal in NFL history.

How did my father get involved? Raymond Perotta was my father's agent. Before the injury which sidelined my father for good, Perotta was responsible for landing him a seven-year contract with the Patriots — so it's easy to see my father felt he owed something to Raymond Perotta.

Perotta saw the difficulties Mbasa Kilu would face, struggling to make his way in a culture that was a world apart from that in which he was raised. Perotta prevailed on Gardner: *Take care of my boy; see to it that Mbasa Kilu has every opportunity to recognize his full potential.* Gardner did that and more. He became Mbasa Kilu's friend, more like an older brother. As much as anything, my father wanted this story to be a testimonial to that friendship.

For Mbasa Kilu's younger years before he came to the U.S., the story evolved from conversations and interviews with Ofi Leiya and Grandmother Nona; and — on two separate trips to Douglastown — with Mbasa Kilu's teachers and friends and members of the Douglastown Leopards.

As for the rest, it is for the most part the story my father told me: what happened from the time Mbasa Kilu's overseas flight arrived at Logan Airport; what happened when he was given a chance to try out for the Patriots; what happened when he made the team; what happened in the season that followed. My father — Gardner — was there for it. Not only was he there, but he was an important part of everything that happened. He told me the story over the years, and I wrote it down. If my father didn't remember the complete story, I wrote down what made sense. I don't mean I invented things — let's say I filled in the blanks. For example, conversations: Who said what? When did they say it? Where were they? Who knows for sure? What I wrote was what made sense.

And I also had a chance to talk with Mbasa Kilu himself — well after his playing days. So some of the story is from his own lips — to the extent I was ever able to get him to talk about it.

Anyway, let's go from there: what happened when Mbasa Kilu's overseas flight arrived at Logan Airport.

* * * * *

Here I should include a dedication, which will become more clear as the story is told:

This book is dedicated to Martin.

* * * * *

A World Apart

Raymond Perotta knew that Mbasa Kilu had never left his home town for more than a few hours, and knew that coming to the U.S. would not be an easy thing, even though he did everything to make it so.

For example, instead of putting Mbasa Kilu at a hotel when he arrived, Perotta — sensing that Mbasa Kilu had never stayed in a hotel — brought him to his own house. Sure enough, Mbasa Kilu had never stayed in a hotel; he had never eaten alone in a restaurant; he had never *been* in a restaurant except for the team banquets at the Great River Inn in Douglastown following their two championship seasons. "It's easier if you just stay with me," said Perotta, "at least until the tryout is over."

And when it was time to go to the New England practice facility, Perotta drove him. This avoided the need for a taxi, which was one other thing Mbasa Kilu had never tried alone.

Some of what he encountered Mbasa Kilu had already seen on ESPN International, which he had watched with the brothers. But in person it was different.

First of all, the practice facility was a good deal larger than even the game stadium in Douglastown. In U.S. football the goal posts had no net, and although the crossbar was at the right height, the uprights extended above. The field was roughly the size of their pitch, as they called it — at least the same length, only wider.

Mbasa Kilu had plenty of time to take this all in after they arrived and parked at the practice facility. Perotta told Mbasa Kilu to wait while he went to speak with someone on the coaching staff. There were dozens of players on the field in groups, going through various drills. Some groups were passing around several U.S. footballs. Others were blocking one another. Others stood and listened as coaches walked them through formations and maneuvers.

When Perotta returned he was with a grey-haired man he introduced as Angelo. "Angelo will take you for your physical," said Perotta. "I'll get you after practice."

Once Angelo took over and headed him for the medical facility, it was the last Mbasa Kilu would see of the practice field for Day One.

* * * * *

After the first hour of the physical, Mbasa Kilu wondered if the kicking tryout would be any harder. He was ushered from one doctor or nurse to another. They took his blood pressure; they drew blood; they listened to his chest and his back; they asked him to close his eyes and stand on one leg. "Muh-Basa," they called him. One even said "McBasa." They asked him questions and keyed his answers into laptops. Before leaving each person, he was asked to sign the screen.

And his feet: each person wanted to know about his feet. How long had they been like this? When were they treated? Why not? It was not possible in the town where he lived, Mbasa Kilu said. He did not say anything about the Great Spirit. He had long since stopped talking about the Great Spirit and his revenge: the White Franciscan Sisters had backed him down from mentioning this, as had Grandmother Nona, even though he still thought it *could* be true — well, he wasn't really sure.

When he was finished with the last person, Angelo appeared again. He said there would be no more practice that day. "You're staying with Mr. Perotta again tonight, right?" At the same moment, Perotta drove up in front of the clinic.

On the way home Perotta wanted to know everything that happened. Mbasa Kilu told him what he remembered about the exams and interviews. "Everybody wanted to know about my feet," he said. He asked Perotta if he might be rejected because of his feet. Perotta reassured him that the questions were routine. "Just kick it like you did back home," he said.

Mrs. Perotta — who told him to call her Helen — greeted Mbasa Kilu after kissing her husband. "How did everything go today?" she asked.

Helen served what she said was meat loaf and mashed potatoes and gravy. The Mission Housekeeper had made meat loaf once when Brother Jerome Jenkins requested it — but only once. Helen's version was actually very good, but for the second night in a row there were no yams, and Mbasa Kilu missed them. He wondered if they had them in the U.S.

* * * * *

After supper, Mbasa Kilu called Grandmother Nona. It was two a.m. when the phone rang in her kitchen. When he heard her sleepy voice he pictured her sitting at the table in her bathrobe. She would be able to reach out and touch the coal oil stove where she cooked. Two meters in the other direction was the cabinet from which he fetched plates and cups when he set the table for their suppers together when he visited. It was the same house he grew up in, the same kitchen where he ate *fufilla* every morning before the van from the White Franciscan Sisters school picked him up.

Grandmother Nona asked if he still had clean clothes. Was he getting enough to eat? What did he have for supper?

Mbasa Kilu told about the meat loaf and mashed potatoes and gravy. Grandmother Nona laughed when he reminded her about Miss Rose's version of meat loaf.

She reminded him to be grateful to Mr. and Mrs. Raymond Perotta — to thank her for the meals. "And get your sleep," she said.

When Grandmother Nona had said that to him at home, he took it for granted. Now Mbasa Kilu felt homesick for Grandmother Nona. After he hung up, he wiped his eyes before leaving the phone.

* * * * *

The Kicking Tryout

No time was wasted on Day Two before Mbasa Kilu was led to a second practice field, away from the rest of the team. Actually, it was simply an empty area behind the temporary grandstand. But it was marked off with chalk like the main field, with goal posts erected at either end. Perotta was left to observe from a distance, looking over the back of the grandstand.

Mbasa Kilu was given time for a few warm-up kicks. This is when he met my father. My father, Gardner, was a friendly man. During the latter part of his career, he considered himself as much a coach as a player, and he dressed that way, partly as a player in his low-cut football shoes, partly as a coach in a white T-shirt and a baseball hat.

"Gardner," he said, holding out his hand. Instructed by Raymond Perotta, Mbasa Kilu took his hand in return, but just to be sure he went through his little pointing ritual — he called it pointing *Good Health!* While Mbasa Kilu was kicking, my father stood nearby, catching the balls as they were returned by an assistant equipment manager standing near the goal post.

"Take some warm-ups," Gardner said. "It may be a while until Doctor Dimples gets off his cell phone." He nodded toward a pudgy coach — the kicking coach, he said — who had walked onto the field with them but was having a phone conversation at the moment.

Mbasa Kilu had trouble getting used to the oval-shaped U.S. football, and his first couple of kicks were a little shaky. Picking up the next ball, Gardner spoke up before handing it to him. "Does Perotta know you hold it this way?" he asked in disbelief. He demonstrated by holding the axis of the ball across his foot, as Mbasa Kilu was doing. "Most kickers hold it the length of their foot," he said, demonstrating again.

Mbasa Kilu explained that he had only kicked a round football. But he tried to hold it the way Gardner demonstrated, and the result was a long, high spiral behind the goal post, over the head of the retriever. His next two warm-up kicks were as good.

Gardner whistled. "Hey, Dimples," he called out to the coach, "you better come over here."

The Patriots' kicking coach measured on a stop watch the amount of time Mbasa Kilu's next two kicks stayed in the air, but didn't write anything on his clipboard. He was measuring what he called "hang time," the longer the better, for it was the time the kicking team had to get down the field and cover the kick. "This can't be right," he said. Finally he marked down the third kick. "Nine point eight," he called out to Gardner. They both knew the NFL record was eight seconds.

Mbasa Kilu got off three more kicks in the nine-plus range before the kicking coach turned toward the grandstand and gave Perotta a thumbs up. They all gathered beside the grandstand when the tryout was over. "He got his physical yesterday," said Perotta, "but he still hasn't done any paper work." He indicated he just needed a standard player contract, one year. "After we see how this year goes, we'll talk about next year." He turned to Mbasa Kilu. "Okay, Champ?"

Mbasa Kilu smiled back. He knew that in the U.S., "champ" stood for "champion." And the champion would be the Super

Bowl champion. Or Mr. Muhammad Ali, said to have been the greatest champion who ever was.

Gardner took him inside to the player personnel office to get his contract prepared. Gardner seemed to know the secretaries in the office, and dictated Mbasa Kilu's answers. Mbasa Kilu was glad when Gardner spoke up and said he would be Mbasa Kilu's roommate. When one of the secretaries raised her eyebrows, Gardner was quick to respond. "What's the matter, Jennifer?" he said. "Do you want to room with us? We can always make room for her, right, Champ?" He clapped Mbasa Kilu on the back.

* * * * *

Mbasa Kilu called Grandmother Nona again that night. He told her he had a job with the Patriots. "At least for now," he said. He said this meant he would not be coming home immediately.

"I know," she said. "Just don't do anything that gets you hurt."

"How is the TV?" he asked. Grandmother Nona started to describe what she had watched the evening before. "How is the *set*?" he asked. She said it was getting dimmer. Mbasa Kilu had replaced parts when he was there to fix it. Now he told her he was sending a money order. There would be enough for a new set, he said. "Mr. Munkasy at the hardware on Maryville Pike will help you find something," he said. He said she could get a ride with the Mission Caretaker, next time he goes. They have not yet hired a new Mission Caretaker, she said. "Then ask Brother Jerome Jenkins," he said. "Next time he goes in town."

He said he missed her yams. He missed *her*.

"I miss you, too," she said. "Be careful."

Whenever Mbasa Kilu talked to her he asked about the TV. There was always an excuse why she didn't have it. She was busy preparing for her friend Cortés's birthday. She had been hanging out wash when Brother Jerome Jenkins came by and couldn't go in her old dress. She had an appointment at the beauty shop the same day he was going to the hardware. No, she didn't want Brother Jerome Jenkins to get a set for her. She would pick it out herself when she had the time. She wanted to have her own choice.

Mbasa Kilu decided not to bother her about it any more.

* * * * *

Each day Gardner had some other things to tell him. He explained that where they played wasn't a pitch, it was a field. "A pitch is in baseball," he said.

"And there's no 'goal,'" Gardner said. "You can kick a *field* goal, but a goal is in hockey. Or soccer."

Mostly the days were spent kicking. Kicking over the goal line. Kicking just short of the goal line. Kicking into the corner. Mostly with Gardner. Sometimes with another player. Once or twice a man named Padrowski — a huge player Gardner referred as the long snapper — would take part and throw the ball to Mbasa Kilu between his legs. Mbasa Kilu had seen this on ESPN. Gardner told him later Padrowski was actually the *backup* long snapper.

Padrowski fired the ball back with intent. At first Mbasa Kilu had trouble catching it. "Ease up," Gardner told Padrowski. "Give him a chance to get used to it." "Heads up," Gardner said to Mbasa Kilu. "Keep your hands up. Keep your eye on the ball." Eventually Mbasa Kilu handled most of the throws from the long snapper. He still dropped one out of seven or eight. "We'll work on that," Gardner said. He started firing the ball to Mbasa Kilu, who got better catching it, but still not perfect.

* * * * *

Once Mbasa Kilu turned around to see the entire team and coaches walking off the field. "Team meeting," said Gardner. "Don't worry about it. No one even knows we're here." Gardner said they would wait till everyone cleared out and then take off for supper.

This was his third night with Gardner. Gardner told him a lot of other things. He took Mbasa Kilu to the bank, set up a checking account and an IRA, arranged to have his checks from the Patriots go directly into the checking account. Mbasa Kilu had occasionally helped Brother Jerome Jenkins pay bills, so this was something he knew. But he had a little trouble with relative amounts. His annual salary as Mission Caretaker had been 10,500,000 tilotas. As a first year rookie with the Patriots, he made only $285,000.

"*Only?*" said Gardner. "Trust me," Gardner told him, "you're getting more."

That night Mbasa Kilu worked it out for himself, saw that Gardner was right. He didn't know anyone in Douglastown — even Mr. Munkasy — who made as much as he was getting from the Patriots.

Gardner did one other thing that was important. He signed Mbasa Kilu up for citizenship classes, which were held two nights a week at the Federal Courthouse in Framingham. If a class had to be missed because the team was on the road, Mbasa Kilu could make it up on-line. Mbasa Kilu was interested in the U.S. Government to begin with. Plus my father knew it would be a benefit to him to be a citizen. Little did he know how much.

When Mr. Raymond Perotta heard that Mbasa Kilu was taking citizenship classes, he persuaded the governor's office to nominate Mbasa Kilu to the FasTrack program under the new immigration law, enabling someone specially designated by a governor or member of Congress to become a citizen in as little as a few months — if he fulfilled all the requirements.

By this stage of his career, Gardner had purchased a large house in a town called Wayland — much larger even than Mr. Munkasy's house in Douglastown — and he gave Mbasa Kilu a bedroom upstairs with a bathroom and shower attached to it.

Gardner drove him back and forth to the practice facility. The first couple of weeks of training camp Gardner and Mbasa Kilu would get something to eat on the way home, then fall asleep exhausted in front of the TV, eventually shuffling off to bed to get a few more hours of sleep before having to roll out again at sunrise the next day.

Gardner showed him how to make coffee in the coffee-maker, and showed him a choice of cereal. There was no fufilla but Mbasa Kilu learned to like the U.S. cereal with milk and sugar — and the coffee, which he would have ready by the time Gardner appeared.

The day their first regular paychecks were deposited Gardner invited him out to Henrietta's on Route 1, where they ate from food set out on the bar and drank a beer called Samuel Adams, after the Second President of the United States, said Mbasa Kilu. (My father laughed when he told me this, but he said the man was actually very smart: knew more about U.S. government than a good many of their teammates, also knew facts about past Super Bowl winners, who coached them, who the quarterbacks were.)

A few other players were at Henrietta's. Soon groups of girls started to arrive, and Mbasa Kilu saw a familiar scene playing out: it was the Mission Picnic, and the girls would stay to one side of the compound, and be careful not to let him see them staring at his feet, and careful not to make eye contact with him, but only with the boys they wished to dance with.

Gardner introduced him to a friend of the girl he was dancing with, who immediately had to gather up her purse and head for the rest room. Anyway, he was not familiar with the dances they were doing, so he sat at the bar and helped himself to the food set out there, and drank another bottle of Samuel Adams, and watched the four TV sets — one of which showed a Premier League game — Fulham vs. Liverpool — real football. After a while Gardner lost interest and they headed home.

The next time the idea of Henrietta's came up, Mbasa Kilu made the excuse that he hadn't slept well the night before, but Gardner should feel free to go himself. After all, he didn't need to go to Henrietta's to watch Premier League football, he could watch this on Gardner's TV.

Occasionally Gardner had a female friend over, and for a while they would watch TV — the three of them — then Gardner and his friend would disappear together, and Mbasa Kilu would slip off to his bedroom upstairs. Once he encountered Gardner's friend in the kitchen when he came downstairs the next morning. She had already made coffee, and set out a mug for him. She asked him how long he had known Gardner, and asked what it was like back home, in Douglastown. He told her about Grandmother Nona, and she said she too had a favorite Grandmother, though she grew up with her mother and father.

(That memory was not supplied by my father or by Mbasa Kilu, but actually by my mother, who remembered it vividly, from the earliest days she knew my father. Despite repeated efforts, she was never able to convince any of her friends to go out with Mbasa Kilu. And if any of them agreed, they would apologize and cancel at the last minute.)

My father was equally unsuccessful in finding a date for Mbasa Kilu. But he told him everything he needed to know to get along in the NFL.

Gardner also told Mbasa Kilu about himself. He was still on the player roster — listed as a second backup quarterback. But inactive. They would only activate him if they needed him. He had been starting quarterback for three full seasons — nine years ago in San Diego — and for stretches of games at other times. But a series of knee injuries eventually sidelined him for good. He would have surgery and rehab and get well from one injury and two games later be hit and knocked out of the lineup again. Finally the team physician sat him down. "I've done everything I can," he said. "The docs in Worcester have given up on you. If you keep this up you'll be in a wheelchair the rest of your life."

So the Patriots finally inactivated him, but kept him around to tutor the young quarterbacks who came along. "You could say I'm sort of a quarterbacks coach, or assistant," he said. Plus at one time he had been the holder for field goal and extra point attempts. He could be re-activated just to do this.

"Speaking of which, have you ever tried place kicking?" Gardner asked him one afternoon. When Gardner explained the difference, Mbasa Kilu was reminded of the unsuccessful attempts to teach him to kick it in the goal back home. There he kicked it off the ground, like what Gardner described as a place kick, where somebody held the ball on the ground or it was placed on a tee on the ground and you kicked.

What Mbasa Kilu had been doing here in the U.S. was called a punt — holding the ball in the air and kicking it. Holding the ball and kicking it was actually illegal back home in real football — unless it was a side kick or you were the goalkeeper clearing the ball. Holding it was just how he learned to kick it playing alone in the lane. He realized Grandmother Nona had taught him that. Gardner said they would try place kicking the next day.

* * * * *

Next day Gardner first put the ball on a tee and did a demonstration kick. "You usually want to kick it away from the returner," he said, pointing to the retriever, who this day was a coach's kid. Gardner kicked it into the other corner. "But not out of bounds," he added.

After a couple of trials, Mbasa Kilu was sending high end-over-end kicks soaring down the field. "Great," said Gardner. "You got the idea." Unlike his teammates back home, Gardner actually liked the way he kicked. Although back home they had been mostly nice about it, he knew they were disappointed he couldn't learn to kick it into the net.

Gardner started to give him spots to aim at. Just over the boy's head. Just short of the boy. In the corner. It felt more natural to Mbasa Kilu the longer he kicked. "How about right down the center," said Gardner. After a couple of trials Mbasa Kilu had that mastered: right down the center, high enough to clear the crossbar on the goal posts.

"I hope there's something in this for me," said Gardner, after summoning the kicking coach. Coach Murka had appeared two or three times when Mbasa Kilu was punting. Gardner insisted on calling him Dimples, but Mbasa Kilu knew him as Coach Murka.

Gardner put Mbasa Kilu through his paces, giving him spots to hit with his kicks. After Mbasa Kilu's first kick right down the center, Murka grunted. "How far back can you do that?" he asked. Gardner backed him up to the 50 yard line, then his own forty, then his own thirty. "How about without the tee," he asked. Gardner held the ball upright. "Just kick it as usual," he told Mbasa Kilu. It wasn't as easy without the tee, but Mbasa Kilu sailed his third kick over the goal posts from his own 45 yard line. "Do it again," said Murka. And Mbasa Kilu did, the ball clearing the goal post crossbar by a meter.

"Do you realize that's a 65-yard field goal?" said Gardner.

"Okay, for Chrissake, so you're a genius," Murka said to Gardner. "It's different with nobody rushing him." "Keep practicing," he told Mbasa Kilu.

* * * * *

The next day Mbasa Kilu was called to the main practice field for the first time. The rest of the team was there — at least a large group they referred to as the special teams. Gardner referred to it as confusion practice. A punter and a long snapper faced the return team, who were there to practice punt returns. The punter was a young man named Bolt — just out of college. He had kicked with Mbasa Kilu the day before, his first day of practice. He was drafted 87th overall to be New England's punter.

"If they get you out there to kick," said Gardner to Mbasa Kilu, "kick it as far as you can."

The special teams coach was trying to straighten out punt return responsibilities. The return team was divided into the left side and the right side, trying to fulfill their blocking responsibilities as the ball sailed downfield. After Bolt's first two punts, it was apparent some members of the return team had different notions of whether they were supposed to be blocking out on the punter's right side or the returner's right side.

Murka motioned Mbasa Kilu onto the field while two different coaches tried to explain blocking assignments. When the return team was finally ready, Mbasa Kilu stood where he had seen Bolt standing, ready to take the snap. He looked toward Gardner on the sideline to see if this was right. When he looked back the ball was already snapped. Mbasa Kilu reached out awkwardly to grab it, but it fell through his fingers to the ground.

"Kick it!" he heard Gardner cry out. Hurriedly he picked up the ball, kicking it off-balance, angling toward the sideline, out of reach of the returner.

Frustrated, the special teams coach shouted at Coach Murka for a decent kick. "Can you kindly get somebody to put it in the vicinity of the returner?" he said.

"Number 21," shouted Gardner to Mbasa Kilu. "The returner is Number 21. Try to hit Number 21." Murka motioned to the long snapper to do it again. "Heads up!" shouted Gardner. This time Mbasa Kilu caught it cleanly, took a wobbly step forward, and kicked.

The ball took off, sailed high over the practice field, and seemed to hang up there, until it finally started to return to earth. Number 21 didn't have to move an inch, but by the time he caught it, the return team was bunched around him, mingled with the kicking team. They all looked dumbfounded, as if they were surprised the ball had actually come down. Coach Murka looked vindicated.

After a couple of seconds of stunned silence, the special teams coach was the first to recover. "What was *that* supposed to be?" he said to Murka. "How the hell are we supposed to practice returns against something like that? Can you get the new kid back in there?" "The college kid," he added, looking toward Bolt.

Mbasa Kilu returned to the sideline beside Gardner. "That's okay," said Gardner. "You got their attention."

* * * * *

Attention, indeed! Reporters in the stands had witnessed Mbasa Kilu's soaring kick, not to mention his crooked gait, the wobbly steps he took. When they brought it up the next day at the head coach's press conference, Coach Buster Dudley professed not to know. "I try to keep my nose out of special teams," he said. "I have enough on my mind without that." "Last I knew Kevin Bolt was our punter," he added, glancing at a depth chart on the podium.

Nevertheless, reporters wanted to get hold of Mbasa Kilu. Gardner appointed himself Mbasa Kilu's press secretary. "He just got to this country," he told the reporters. "He isn't ready for interviews yet. Let him nail down a job first, get a spot on the roster."

Gardner had an answer for everything the reporters asked. "Kilu," he told them. "K — I — L — U." "Douglastown," he said. "Just like it sounds." "The Douglastown *Journal,* I suppose." "Or *Times.* Why don't you look it up?" "Did you guys ever hear of research?" he asked, putting them off. "Maybe if you stopped playing games on your Blackberries and did some research you wouldn't have all these ignorant questions."

And the special teams coaches paid attention. Bolt continued to kick for return practice, but Mbasa Kilu was brought back into punting practice. On the practice field, they punted side by side. "Call me Kevin," said Bolt, who like his teammates called Mbasa Kilu "*Muh-*Basa." Gardner was one of the only people who said "*Em-*Basa." Mbasa Kilu learned to answer to both.

Three days before the first exhibition game (against the Eagles), Coach Murka told Mbasa Kilu he would be put in for a punt or two. The first chance came near the end of the half. The game was already showing the raggedness of a first exhibition game. By then the Eagles had turned over three fumbles; the Patriots were plagued by broken running plays and incomplete passes. Neither offense had really gotten started; neither had scored. Bolt had handled his three punts with credit. Once again the Patriots were stuck on their own 32, with fourth down and long yardage. Murka motioned Mbasa Kilu onto the field with the punting team. Bolt stayed on the sideline and watched.

The crowd was becoming inattentive, but Gardner shouted out his instructions: "Heads up!" he said. "Keep your eye on the ball." Startled by the charge of the Eagle line, Mbasa Kilu briefly bobbled the pass from center, hurriedly kicked after half a wobbly step. The ball angled toward the sideline, out of bounds only twenty yards downfield. Only a last-second block by Number 34 Cook kept the kick from being blocked. Mbasa Kilu thanked him, as Gardner had told him to do. "No problem, Bro," Cook answered. "Don't worry about those guys. We'll keep them away from you," he said. "Just lay into that sucker and kick it." Then he added, "And if anyone so much as touches you, fall down and play dead."

Mbasa Kilu got another chance in the third quarter. This time he tried to follow Cook's advice, not worry about the charging line. Kicking from his own 15, Mbasa Kilu sailed the ball well into Eagle territory, where the Eagle returner signaled a fair catch, only to have the ball land ten yards behind him, downed by Number 89 Porter on the Eagle 11.

"Field position," said the Patriot announcer. *"That's what I call field position!"* *"Believe me,"* he added, *"if the Patriots can't move the ball any better than they have today, they'll need all the field position they can scrape up."*

The game ended with the Eagles ahead of the Patriots, 21-13. After Mbasa Kilu's two attempts, Kevin Bolt had handled the rest of the punts creditably. But two different Patriot place kickers managed only two of five field goal attempts. On Sunday the *Boston Globe* was quick to point out that the Patriots' kicking woes, a problem for the last three seasons, seemed anything but solved. The three missed field goals were the margin of defeat.

"They're not talking about you," Gardner said. "It's that four-million dollar genius they got from the Falcons," he said, "who can't kick a field goal from beyond thirty-five yards." No, Gardner told him when Mbasa Kilu asked, he shouldn't apologize to Coach Murka for bobbling the first of his two punt attempts. "Nobody's worried about punts," said Gardner. "The problem is touchdowns and field goals."

* * * * *

Practice on Monday focused on field goals. The field goal team practiced with both kickers, who nailed kicks from 40 and 50 yards. It was in the actual games where it all seemed to slip away. Gardner watched for awhile before returning to the auxiliary practice field, where Kevin Bolt and Mbasa Kilu were practicing punts. He arranged with Bolt to split the field, Bolt practicing his punts off to one side, Gardner and Mbasa Kilu practicing field goals straight down the middle. "This will be different at first," Gardner told Mbasa Kilu, "But you'll get it." He summoned three of the coaches' kids, one to retrieve for Bolt, one to retrieve for Mbasa Kilu, one to act as long snapper. "Just throw it to me," Gardner told the kid. "Don't try to snap it," he said, "just toss it back to me."

They started from the 35 yard line, Gardner on one knee seven yards back. First Gardner had Mbasa Kilu stand three steps farther back and two and one half steps to the side. When he saw the effect of Mbasa Kilu's wobbly stride, how short it was, he brought him up closer, two steps back from him. The kid would toss it to Gardner. who would catch the ball and place it down. Mbasa Kilu would take a wobbly step forward and kick it.

Mbasa Kilu had no trouble kicking it as far as the goal, over the goal, and between the uprights. Gardner saw that the step forward needed the work — not so much that it was wobbly, but the timing. Mbasa Kilu was waiting too long. "Try to antic-ipate where the ball will be," said Gardner, "so you can kick it the instant I put it down."

Soon Mbasa Kilu started to master the steps, started to kick as soon as Gardner put it down. "You're a natural," Gardner told him. "Let's go back to the 45."

There it was the same: Mbasa Kilu's kicks were sailing way over the goal post, and dead center. From the 50 it was the same. Only when they got to the opposite 45 yard line did Mbasa Kilu start to miss, and even there he was hitting three out of four dead center.

Gardner sent the kid to fetch Coach Murka, then set the ball up on the closer 40 yard line.

"Why is he standing on top of you like that?" Murka asked. Gardner told about moving him up to accommodate his shorter stride. "But then he'll start on the wrong foot," said Murka. "This is what happens when a washed-up quarterback tries to do a coach's job," he said. "You've taught him the wrong foot."

"Who cares?" said Gardner. "You try kicking with feet like his," he said, "and see what foot you start on." Mbasa Kilu was embarrassed at the talk about his feet, and more embarrassed to see Gardner arguing with the coach. For an instant he wanted to practice punting with Bolt. But he noticed Bolt and his retriever had stopped and were watching.

"That doesn't make it right," said Murka, "but go ahead."

Gardner started with the ball on the 40 yard line, and knelt seven yards back, then motioned to the kid to start. The kid tossed him the ball, he placed it down. Mbasa Kilu took his wobbly step forward and kicked. The ball sailed over the goal posts and well beyond, bouncing against the chain link fence at the boundary of the property. They did it again, and a third time — all good kicks.

Gardner backed up the operation first to the 45, then to midfield, with equal success. Finally, kicking from his own territory, Mbasa Kilu missed, but nevertheless made two out of four.

"I can see some potential," said Murka, still not happy with Gardner's intruding into his area. "He's got the leg okay," he told Gardner. "Where he gets it I don't know. But he's still pretty unsteady," he added. He turned to Mbasa Kilu. "Good work, Kilu," he said. "Keep practicing."

"Don't forget," he told Gardner, "we signed him as a punter." He added that they were already paying big money for two placekickers, and didn't need a third. "Unless somebody gets injured," he added, as if he were planning it out then and there.

* * * * *

Neither of the placekickers was injured in the preseason, though the backup was given his unconditional release before the season started. The placekicker Gardner nicknamed the Four-Million Dollar Genius started to find his range, managing seven field goals in nine attempts — not spectacular but at least not embarrassing.

As for punting, Kevin Bolt remained the number one punter, but Mbasa Kilu got an opportunity in each of the three remaining preseason games. Once he briefly bobbled the snap from center and looped a weak kick toward the sideline. The other five times he sent soaring kicks into corners of the field where his teammates downed them deep in the opposing team's territory.

By the beginning of the season Mbasa Kilu had established himself as a member of the team. He was listed on the program as a punter, just after Kevin Bolt:

#8 — Bolt, Kevin — P

#9 — Kilu, Mbasa — P

Only Murka and Gardner knew of his place-kicking ability — and Kevin Bolt, who practiced punts beside him. In addition to punts, Gardner had him practice place-kicking every chance he got, explaining the rules of kickoffs and extra points and field goals. Meanwhile, the Four-Million Dollar Genius was listed as the placekicker, handling field goals, extra points, and kickoffs, achieving more of the promise he showed when he was signed by the team.

* * * * *

Once during the season near the end of practice it started to rain — hard. Hard enough that the coaches whistled an end to the day's drills. Players ran for the locker rooms, coaches not far behind. Mbasa Kilu noticed that practice balls were spread far and wide outside the sideline, ball boys and the equipment manager scrambling to gather them in the big canvas bag. He bent and picked up the four balls nearest him and took them to the bag. While a surprised ball boy held the bag open he tossed the balls in, and for an instant he felt like he was on the practice pitch in Douglastown, picking up after practice.

In that instant he felt a wave of homesickness. He turned his head away so no one would notice his eyes tearing up, and took his time going back to the locker room.

Sometimes in the days following he wondered if perhaps the practice pitch in Douglastown was where he belonged, not here on a U.S. football team. He would feel homesick for that other life. Would he ever get back to it? But in the crowded days living with Gardner — daily practice, trips every couple of weeks, exhaustion at night — there was little time for homesickness.

* * * * *

Mbasa Kilu's first chance as a placekicker came against the Falcons in the third game of the season. The Four-Million Dollar Genius — who was a field goal specialist — kicked off to start the game, a weak kick returned to midfield by the Falcons, who easily marched in from there for a touchdown in four plays. In the second quarter the Falcons took a 14-0 lead before the Patriots managed a field goal to make it 14-3. After kicking the field goal, the Four-Million-Dollar Genius sent the kickoff angling out of bounds, resulting in a penalty which allowed the Falcons to start from their own 40. The special teams coach seethed: an out-of-bounds kickoff was a No-No — a wasteful concession of field position. Murka spoke to the kicker as he left the field, but the Four-Million-Dollar Genius didn't even stop to listen, heading instead to get a drink. Some of this was caught on the scoreboard video screen, and the special teams coach and Murka exchanged looks.

There were no more placekicking opportunities until the third period. By then the Falcons extended the lead to 28-3, and were driving for a fifth touchdown when number 34 Cook intercepted a pass and ran 72 yards for a Patriots touchdown. It was the first defensive touchdown of the season, and the Patriots defensive players mobbed Cook in the end zone, indulging in a celebration worthy of the occasion — and worthy of a penalty flag, this time fifteen yards for unsportsmanlike conduct — excessive celebration. This meant the Patriots would have to kick off from deep in their own territory — from their 15-yard line instead of the 30.

The special teams coach huddled with Coach Murka. "Where's that punter from wherever that you say place kicks a mile?" he asked. "Why don't you give him a chance?" Murka motioned to Mbasa Kilu, who had already been alerted by Gardner. "It's 15 yards farther," Gardner told him, "so kick it harder — but try not to put it over the goal line." Kevin Bolt smacked him on the behind. "Give 'em hell, Mbasa," he said. "Show them how a punter does it."

When he took the field with the kickoff team, Mbasa Kilu realized he couldn't even *see* the opposing goal line from where he was, but he knew it was just a few meters short of the white goal posts beyond. He realized something else about kickoffs that hadn't occurred to him before — the ball was on the tee — and he didn't have to catch it before kicking. Mbasa Kilu backed up from the ball the way Gardner had showed him, and waited for the referee's whistle. Somehow the kicking team remained onside as he advanced his wobbly steps toward the ball.

The kick was so high it seemed about to go out of sight. The Falcons' two returners pointed to one another, before one finally camped under the ball on his own three yard line, signaling a fair catch. The Falcons' sideline screamed at him to let it go across the goal line, but by the time he realized, he had already caught it and downed it on the four.

Members of the kicking team smacked Mbasa Kilu on the helmet as they left the field. Coaches shouted encouragement. Coach Murka extended his hand and congratulated him. "Way to go, Kilu," he said. Gardner — uncharacteristically speechless — grabbed him around the shoulders and held on.

Unable to advance the ball, the Falcons had to punt from their own end zone. The exchange of field position resulted in another Patriot touchdown, although the Falcons still won convincingly, 45-24.

Next morning the *Globe* Sports Page bemoaned the Patriots' second loss in three games, but an item in the *Pats Chat* column on page 6 of the sports section mentioned the kick, under the heading *Mboomer!* "On a day when there was little else to cheer about, the Patriots trotted out a newly signed kicker named Mbasa Kilu, who astounded fans with a booming 81-yard kickoff, pinning the Falcons against their own goal line and ultimately resulting in a touchdown. Kilu, who walks with difficulty as a result of deformed feet, is listed on the roster as a backup punter to rookie sensation Kevin Bolt. Though he did not punt, he sent writers scrambling for the record books to determine the longest kickoff without a return — for which there are no statistics."

* * * * *

From then on Mbasa Kilu was "Boomer" to most of his teammates, though Gardner still called him "Mbasa." On Tuesday reporters talked about the kick, and once again Gardner took the questions for Mbasa Kilu. "What do you mean, has he ever kicked it this far?" he said. "He never participated in an actual game until the preseason, and you saw that. And this was his first kickoff. Back home he was equipment manager for a soccer team, so go figure." Eventually they prevailed on Gardner to let Mbasa Kilu answer a question himself. "Who taught you to kick like that?" a Peabody weekly *News* reporter asked. When Mbasa Kilu answered that his Grandmother Nona taught him, some of the reporters couldn't suppress their laughter. Gardner stepped back in. "Not literally," said Gardner, who had heard the story of Mbasa Kilu's kicking in the lane. "What he means is — he was home schooled. He did this every day at recess. If you guys knew the first thing about different cultures, you wouldn't find this so funny."

The next day five different versions of the story appeared. The *Globe* summed it up. "Mbasa Kilu — whose record-breaking kickoff earned him the nickname 'Boomer' with his teammates — is only a second string punter on the Patriots roster, but that should change before long."

* * * * *

It did not change immediately. Mbasa Kilu continued to see action only during practice, and there mostly as a punter, methodically kicking his high arching kicks beside Kevin Bolt. Mbasa Kilu still had occasional trouble handling the snap from center, despite repeated practice sessions conducted by Gardner. He also was distracted by the charging line — not only as a punter but as a field goal kicker.

But kickoffs involved neither of these elements, and the special teams coach and Coach Murka resolved to find a way that Mbasa Kilu's phenomenal ability could better their kickoff efforts.

They changed the Four-Million-Dollar Genius from a place-kicking specialist into a field goal and extra point specialist. Mbasa Kilu would handle kickoffs. And Kevin Bolt was more than able to handle punting duties by himself.

Meanwhile, they worked Mbasa Kilu out with the kickoff team. He didn't need to practice the kicks, only to hear where the special teams coach wanted him to kick it. Gardner would shout out the directions from the special teams coach — "left corner," "right corner," "down the middle." At first they tried to give Mbasa Kilu a path to run down the field, then realized that with his wobbly gait he was unlikely to contribute anything beyond the kick. "We got your back, Bro," number 34 Cook told him, "just put that sucker up there and watch what happens."

What happened in practice is that most of his kicks came down inside the receiving team's 10 yard line — and then only after an interminably high arc, preventing a runback and giving the kicking team time to surround the return men, forcing them to fair catch and down it deep in their own territory.

Mbasa Kilu took the field with the kickoff team at the beginning of the sixth game of the season — against Pittsburgh. He duplicated his previous spectacular kick, sailing the ball high above the field. By the time it came down, half the Patriots' kickoff team was around the return men, forcing the Steelers to fair catch and down the ball inside their own 10 yard line.

Mbasa Kilu repeated this five more times against Pittsburgh. Facing these kickoffs and effective punts by Kevin Bolt, the Steelers spent the afternoon struggling to get out of their own territory. The Patriots worked this to their advantage, 23-14, winning their third game of the season. By the end of the game shouts of "Boomer!" greeted Mbasa Kilu when he took the field.

The win seemed to convince the Patriots that they were a team to be reckoned with, a feeling that stayed with them to the end of the season. Even the lukewarm Patriot offense heated up.

* * * * *

As for Mbasa Kilu, my father was never able to get over the fact that he took it all for granted.

"He didn't seem to understand what all the excitement was about," he said. Mbasa Kilu even asked Gardner whether the cries of "Boomer" were a compliment.

"*Compliment!?*" said my father. "You bet it's a compliment." He told Mbasa Kilu the fans had never witnessed kickoffs like he was doing on a routine basis.

With the Pittsburgh win came a deluge of fan reaction — cards, letters, faxes, e-mails. After watching Mbasa Kilu painfully composing a response to the first couple of messages, Gardner convinced him to let the Patriots Public Relations office answer for him. If an address was specified, they also sent a photo: Mbasa Kilu from the waist up, preparing to punt — "heads up" stance, hands poised to receive the snap from center.

* * * * *

That fall the weather was an ally to the Patriots — turning severe from mid-October. Home games at the aging Gillette Stadium were played in cold rain and eventually 25-mile winds and blowing snow. Mbasa Kilu was used to rain, but not to cold weather, much less this cold. Nevertheless he launched his soaring kickoffs time after time, causing the opposing teams to start from deep in their own territory. He did even better when games were played in opponents' stadiums, especially those indoors.

It was at one of those indoor games, in Detroit, that Mbasa Kilu got his first opportunity to kick a field goal. Gardner had talked Coach Murka into letting Mbasa Kilu practice long-range field goals with the regular holder and long snapper. Then he managed to sell the head coach and the special teams coaches on the idea of letting Mbasa Kilu try field goals that were out of range for the Four-Million-Dollar Genius with time expiring in the half. "Rather than just letting time run out," he argued, "let him take a shot. Field position won't be a problem if he misses." The Four-Million-Dollar Genius was more than happy to share duties: he didn't want to be charged with any long-range misses.

The first opportunity to try out Mbasa Kilu's new role occurred already in the next game. The Patriots were leading the Lions with time about to expire in the first half. A Patriots drive was stalled around the opponents' 41 yard line. Fans — expecting the Patriots would let the clock expire — were already heading to the concession stands. But the Patriot sideline signaled a time out.

"Let's get your long kicker out there," the coach said to Murka. "It's a chance to try him out," he said. "If he misses: he misses."

He didn't miss. The two officials at the goal posts watched as Mbasa Kilu's nearly 60-yard kick rose high above the field before descending through the uprights, giving the Patriots an additional three points at halftime. Then, in a rare show of strength, the Patriot offense continued to dominate the game in the second half — including three field goals by the Four-Million-Dollar Genius from shorter ranges. The Patriots won.

After the game the media response rose to a frenzy. Coach Murka was uncharacteristically in the center of post-game interviews. Mbasa Kilu was also brought in and seated at the interview microphones. Gardner sat beside him and answered most of the questions.

"Nobody really *likes* talking to the press," my father told me. "But the damnedest thing about Mbasa was he couldn't seem to get stirred up about it." After all, the players in Douglastown enjoyed the novelty of his towering kicks, even cheered him on. But that's all they were: a novelty.

On Wednesday the *Boston Globe* ran a photo of Mbasa Kilu and the Four-Million-Dollar Genius — each holding a football — over the caption: *The Long and the Short of It.* Before the season was over Mbasa Kilu twice more kicked field goals from near record-breaking ranges. In addition, he continued to trap the opposing teams deep within their territory with his soaring kickoffs.

As for the rest of the team, Kevin Bolt turned in a fine rookie year as a punter. Number 34 Cook went on to intercept a total of 12 passes, two of which he returned for touchdowns. And the Four-Million Dollar Genius remained in the groove, hitting his last 11 field goals in a row. The offense still struggled, but they too seemed to take heart, raising their average points per game above 20.

And a strange phenomenon occurred: in games on the road, hostile partisan fans continued their rabid behavior in support of the home team. But Mbasa Kilu's short stature and wobbling gate made him stand out from the rest of the players, and without fail the crowds on the road would greet Mbasa Kilu with shouts of "Boomer!" when he took the field.

After the mediocre start, the Patriots seemed to feed on the strength of Mbasa Kilu's record-length field goals. They won seven more times out of the remaining ten games, finishing with ten wins and six losses, making the playoffs for the first time since the Patriot Super Bowl teams of the early 2000s.

Section 5 — The Playoff Game

If the New England players thought the New England weather had been bad that season, it was only because they had yet to play in Green Bay in January.

The temperature hovered just below 20 degrees. Gale force winds blew in off the lake, downing two historic trees at Bay Beach park, picking shingles off the press box atop Lombardi Stadium and sending them spinning wildly through the atmosphere. Out-of-town reporters were unanimously critical of Green Bay management for erecting another outdoor stadium in the 2020s to replace the crumbling Lambeau Field. Only the Green Bay writers were supportive, calling the day "Packer weather."

Mbasa Kilu put his heavy team parka aside long enough to kick the opening kickoff, then retreated to the bench while frozen-faced linemen battled one another to a standstill. For the first time that season Green Bay was held scoreless for the first half. But New England managed no better.

The scoreless standoff continued into the third quarter. The first scoring opportunity occurred near the end of the quarter. Green Bay — unable to make any progress into the wind — hung up a desperate punt that was almost blown backward, giving New England their first opportunity on the opponents' end of the field — starting on the Green Bay 40, operating with the wind in their favor. A running play made no progress. On the next play the New England right tackle — number 78 Higgins — was flagged for unnecessary roughness, the penalty pushing the ball back into New England territory. Two passes fell incomplete, bringing up fourth down with three seconds remaining in the quarter.

A timeout was called and the New England coaches huddled. The consensus among the assistants was to punt, taking advantage of the favorable wind to push Green Bay once again deep into their own territory.

But head coach Buster Dudley was unsatisfied. "What? We punt and hope for a fumble?" he said. "This is getting us nowhere. We might as well pack up and go home."

He turned to Coach Murka. "Your backup boy," he said, "can he hit it from this far out?"

Murka was taken aback: he looked surprised — and doubtful. "A field goal?" he said. "This would be 60, 70, 72 yards."

"He's got a hell of a wind at his back," said the special teams coach. "That ought to be worth 10 or 15 yards."

By now Gardner was already in action, helping Mbasa Kilu get out of his bulky parka. "Just put it right down the middle, Mbasa," he said. "Same as usual."

When the special teams coach ordered the field goal team onto the field, someone had to actually track down the holder: they found him huddled in front of a heater. Nobody expected a field goal attempt from this far away, and in a tie game. When the fans saw Mbasa Kilu take the field in his wobbling gait, they assumed he was coming in to punt in place of Kevin Bolt, the regular punter. But then when the holder knelt to take the snap on his own 38 yard line, indicating a field goal attempt, a murmur of incredulity swept through the crowd. Not only would this be the longest field goal in NFL history — if successful — but it would top the previous record by nine yards. Green Bay, expecting some kind of trick, called time out.

Meanwhile the press box exploded in a flurry of excitement. Why coach Buster Dudley was right to try it. Why he was wrong. The consequences of a missed attempt. The consequences of a made attempt. The worst coaching decision ever made. The best. What effect the wind would have. The record for the longest field goal ever made. The fact that one of the previous record-holders was also physically handicapped. *If coach Buster Dudley has called this one wrong,* rattled the play-by-play announcer, *and the kick is missed, it would give Green Bay the ball in New England territory. And what is the likelihood of making a field goal from this distance?* he added.

Except for an occasional shout of "Boomer!" and the noise of the wind and the flapping of the flags around the periphery of the Green Bay stadium, everything became strangely quiet, a murmur spreading through the crowd.

Mbasa Kilu remained facing the goal posts during the time out, the howling wind at his back. As long as he didn't turn around, he could stand the cold. His teammates said nothing to him, avoided eye contact. The holder got up and smacked him on the butt, but said nothing.

Standing alone in the middle of the field, Mbasa Kilu looked toward the goal posts, to the scoreboard beyond. Score: Green Bay 0, New England 0, Quarter: 3, Time: 0:03. He imagined kicking at the sunny practice field in New England, before the season started. He imagined kicking after practice on the pitch back home. He imagined kicking at the great oak tree. He imagined kicking in the lane. He imagined kicking in his back yard.

The referee's whistle ended the timeout. Mbasa Kilu measured his shortened stride back from the kneeling holder, waited for the snap. The ball was handled cleanly, placed down. Mbasa Kilu took his one wobbly step into the kick. The ball took off like a rocket, pushed by the wind, a high, hanging kick. When it reached the top of its arc it seemed to stop momentarily before plummeting down. It stayed dead center, reached the goal posts and sailed well beyond, hitting the net over the first row of end zone seats. Both referees extended their arms in the air as the third quarter time ran out. Score: Green Bay 0, New England 3, Quarter: 3, Time: 0:00. Teammates mobbed Mbasa Kilu, and he thanked them one by one as Gardner had told him.

Mbasa Kilu made it all the way to the sideline before he realized he had to go right back out and kick off next. When he turned to go back on the field two things had changed. The scoreboard had changed to indicate the beginning of the fourth quarter with New England now holding a slim lead, 3-0. And the teams had changed ends of the field. Mbasa Kilu would kick off into the teeth of the wind.

The Kickoff

Before he even headed back onto the field, Murka and Gardner huddled with him on the sideline. "Just sail it back there, Kilu," said Murka. "Nobody's going anywhere in this mess." Lining up for the kickoff, facing now into the wind, Mbasa Kilu could barely remain standing. Number 34 Cook shouted encouragement. "One more good one, Boomer," he shouted. "Then leave it to us."

Now the gale force wind was laced with a fine sleet that cut into the skin. Paper cups and wrappers swirled around the field. The ball blew off the tee twice before a member of the special teams stooped to hold it. Mbasa Kilu's feet — already plagued with bad circulation — had gone numb. He took one last look at the ball before raising his right hand to signal ready. The referee's whistle blew. The line advanced.

When Mbasa Kilu's foot hit the ball, he knew he had made a solid kick. It didn't sting his foot, as it might have. Instead, he felt blood return to his foot. He felt his whole foot contact the ball. It felt solid. It sounded solid.

The ball sailed into the teeth of the wind, through the sleet and snow, rising into the atmosphere. The kicking team got down the field quickly. Green Bay blockers retreated to form a wedge around the returner, knowing that there was usually no return of an Mbasa Kilu kickoff.

Meanwhile the ball sailed higher, hung in the air longer, held up by the blowing wind currents. It looked at first like it would be into the end zone, giving Green Bay the ball on the 20 yard line. Then, even better, it looked as if it might land on the field of play, just short of the goal line, having to be downed by Green Bay deep in their own territory, with the New England kicking team already waiting underneath.

Just when it looked like it would go New England's way, the laws of nature were suspended. The height of Mbasa Kilu's kick, usually an asset, today held the ball up in the air like a light-weight glider. Instead of dropping toward the Green Bay goal line, the ball lost its forward momentum and — carried by the wind — started to descend in the opposite direction.

For an instant both teams stood frozen in place. Then the Green Bay returner noticed the ball's reverse arc and started to run forward. A split second later Number 34 Cook saw what was happening and set out in pursuit. Other New England players, not accustomed to facing a live kickoff return, were first taken aback, then set off to join the race. At that point the predominantly Green Bay fans got the picture, sending up a sudden roar.

Mbasa Kilu — standing at his own 40 yard line — looked on with horror as the trajectory of the ball started backing up toward him. The Green Bay returner caught it in full stride at his own 25 yard line and headed downfield, with Number 34 Cook one stride behind. When he saw Cook behind him, the returner cut toward the sideline to get away, right toward where Mbasa Kilu still stood.

No one had ever really taught Mbasa Kilu what to do in this case. But he knew one thing — the same thing every one of the screaming Green Bay fans knew — if that runner returned it for a touchdown it would immediately wipe out the slim 3-0 advantage that had just been posted — and probably put the otherwise stalemated game out of reach.

In the seconds which elapsed while the Green Bay returner was closing on him, Mbasa Kilu tried to get an angle on the runner to knock him out of bounds. But before that could happen, just as the Green Bay runner was reaching out to stiff-arm Mbasa Kilu, Cook caught up with the runner from behind. As a result all three collided and went down together in a tangled heap.

Not used to any contact, much less to a collision with two players going at top speed, Mbasa Kilu felt first the impact, then a sharp pain in his kicking foot. Then, when the three of them hit the ground together and rolled over, Mbasa Kilu felt the other ankle snap.

The first to get up from the pile was Cook. He in turn pulled the Green Bay returner off Mbasa Kilu. At the time, the thing Mbasa Kilu was most conscious of was the blinding pain. Later he would remember the referee holding the ball, looking down at where he lay, then signaling to the New England bench for help.

Section 6 — Sidelined

Gardner rode in the front of the ambulance to St. Vincent Hospital and was there when Mbasa Kilu woke up after a six-hour surgery. Actually, waking up took a good deal of time, while he went in and out of sleep.

The doctor who headed the surgical team had spoken to Gardner in the waiting room. He introduced himself as Doctor O'Brien, said the surgery had gone without a hitch — especially in view of everything that had to be done. "Obviously he's finished with football for this year, and then some," he said. The ankle was straightforward, he said, calling the fracture a name Gardner couldn't remember. It was being held with a simple splint, he said, which allowed them to work on the fractures of both feet. "In a word," he said, "the left foot was shattered." Gardner gathered that the right foot was broken but less so, because the ankle on that side was broken, and the ankle took some of the impact. Thinking about it made him woozy. He tried not to pay attention to details as the surgeon described the myriad pins, plates, and screws with which they had pieced together Mbasa Kilu's shattered feet and ankles.

Eventually Gardner signaled *enough*. "I get the general idea," he said.

"At least the club feet have been corrected," said the surgeon. "When he learns to walk again, he'll be walking solidly on the bottoms of his feet." In the meantime the only thing to do was wait, heal, and try to control the pain.

When Mbasa Kilu did finally come full awake, the only thing he seemed to be aware of was the pain. Gardner showed him the analgesia pump, which he immediately tried, and soon again was dozing in and out of consciousness.

The middle-aged man in the next bed had been watching the game wrap-up, which Gardner had seen a half dozen times in the surgery waiting room. It showed Mbasa Kilu's record field goal at the end of the third quarter. It showed the ensuing kickoff, the game-saving tackle by Number 34 Cook, which brought down Mbasa Kilu as well as the runner. It showed Mbasa Kilu's being removed from the field on a cart and taken away in an ambulance. It showed the teams slugging it out in the final minutes in a blinding snow storm. It showed Green Bay advancing into New England territory with two minutes left. It showed Number 34 Cook intercepting a third down pass for New England to cut off the Green Bay drive. Then it showed the final scoreboard - Score: Green Bay 0, New England 3, Quarter: 4, Time: 0:00.

Outside, snow still blew sideways. It had long since turned dark. Visiting hours were over. Mbasa Kilu was sleeping soundly. Gardner wrote his name and phone number on a slip of paper and gave it to the roommate. "Call if anything comes up," he said.

The roommate said he would. "I've been a loyal Packer fan for over 50 years," he said, "but I'm sorry about your friend," nodding toward Mbasa Kilu. "I'll say this: he's one hell of a sleeper," he said.

Gardner also left his name and phone number at the nurse's station, telling them that Mbasa Kilu was still asleep, hadn't used the analgesia pump for two hours — since he was last awake. The nurse nodded. "There are pain meds in the IV for the first 24 hours," she said, "Right now the pump is mostly to give him a sense of control." She said he might sleep through the night.

When Gardner reached the hotel room, he thought of Grandmother Nona. Mbasa Kilu had given Gardner her number the first time he called her. Gardner didn't know what time it would be in Douglastown, but he called anyway. She answered immediately. She had not heard of Mbasa Kilu's injury, but she seemed to take it in stride and was glad to hear he was okay. Gardner said that the doctor thought the surgery on his feet and ankle was successful. He wasn't sure she understood the word ankle, but she understood feet. "He's had that problem since birth," she said. Gardner let it go at that, thinking it was probably better for her that she didn't completely understand. "Just as long as he's okay," she said. "Tell him I've got the new TV," she said. "And tell him that I love him," she added. She thanked Gardner for calling.

* * * * *

Gardner's phone in the hotel room started ringing at 8am.

First it was the team physician, who had talked with the surgeon. Jim O'Brien, he called him. "Do you want a summary of what he did to Kilu's feet?" he asked.

Gardner declined, saying he had gotten all he could take outside the operating room.

"I talked with Austin White at Mass General," the doc said. "Turns out O'Brien trained under him. White and O'Brien both say Kilu should stay put. We shouldn't even think about moving him until he's back on his feet. And that will be months, not weeks." The team physician said he would stay behind for an extra day to make sure all the arrangements were made.

The second call was from the Patriots traveling secretary. The team bus was leaving for the airport at 11:30. Gardner arranged to stay an extra day.

Just after ten the Green Bay Packer fan roommate called. "The minute you left last night he woke up and asked when supper was. Ten o'clock at night he wanted supper! I rang my bell for him, and the nurse fixed him a sandwich, and he went right back to sleep."

Gardner asked if Mbasa was awake yet. He was awake, but had been taken for X-rays. "The docs were in at 7:30 — half a dozen of them," said the roommate. "Then an hour ago a black guy and a fat guy came in." *Cook and Murka,* thought Gardner. "The black guy gave him a football," said the roommate. "And gave me his autograph." He told Gardner he wouldn't have asked for a New England player's autograph, except for his grandson in New Hampshire.

* * * * *

Later that afternoon Mbasa Kilu was able to talk to his roommate, who showed him how to view replays from the game on his bedside TV. He remembered standing in the middle of the field with his back to the wind, which was almost blowing him over. But Mbasa Kilu had an incomplete memory of the plays as they unfolded. He remembered the record-setting field goal. He could not remember the subsequent kickoff, the three-man collision, the exact instant of the injury. Only the pain he felt in both feet confirmed the injury.

He remembered rolling through huge glass doors on a stretcher, and Gardner's voice — out of sight — up ahead of him. Then having something to eat, in the hospital bed. And here he was.

* * * * *

By the following week Mbasa Kilu was able to watch New England's playoff journey come to an end. Playing in the sunshine at Tampa Bay, they put up seven points early, then managed only a field goal the rest of the way. Kevin Bolt handled all his punts well. Even the Four-Million-Dollar Genius performed — keeping all his kickoffs in bounds, converting his only field goal attempt. But the offense faltered, turning the ball over four times, managing only four of eleven third down conversions. Result: Tampa Bay 21, New England 10.

A week after Mbasa Kilu's season was abruptly ended the entire team was headed home.

The following week Mbasa Kilu was moved to the Vince Lombardi Rehabilitation Wing of the hospital, and his new season began.

* * * * *

The first personal mail from home arrived the same week, forwarded from the team headquarters in Boston. It was from Grandmother Nona's friend Gladys. "Speedy Recovery," it said, and Gladys had written in "Handsome." Brother Jerome Jenkins also sent a card, with assurances of prayer for his recovery. Other brothers had signed it, some adding a word or two. Members of the Douglastown Leopards also sent a card with their signatures. "Good Luck!" it said across the top. "Give It a Ride, Mbasa Kilu!" had been filled in below that. The picture showed a soccer player kicking a goal past a diving keeper. Someone had sketched his number "9" on the player's shirt.

Finally there was a blue envelope that smelled like flowers. The card showed a garden and a bird bath and two birds frolicking in the water. Mbasa Kilu read the words "Love, Ofi Leiya and Martin" in Ofi Leiya's neat handwriting. On the back Martin had drawn and colored a tree with red fruit on it.

Mbasa Kilu put her card away in the drawer of his night stand. Every day he took it out and read it.

* * * * *

When Mbasa Kilu tried to reply to Ofi Leiya's card, five times he got as far as "thank you for the card," then said something he didn't wish to say and had to tear it up and start over. Finally he managed to compliment Martin's drawing and add that his feet were getting better every day. Then there was the ending: "Yours truly?" "Best wishes?" Or just nothing except "Mbasa Kilu?" Surely he couldn't just write "Love."

One of the nurses found him writing and rewriting the note. "That must be *some* letter," she said. "You were working on it two days ago."

He explained about "Love" and "Best wishes" and so on. "Which would *you* rather read?" he asked.

"How did she sign *her* letter?" the nurse asked.

He showed her the blue card.

"Seems pretty plain to me," she said. "She said it: Love. By the way, who's Martin?" He explained about Martin and Tedu Ngraeba.

"So," she said. "So she's a widow. Why don't you write 'Love to you and Martin?'"

And, finally, that is how he signed the note to Ofi Leiya.

* * * * *

Needless to say, they had followed the career of Mbasa Kilu back home — to the extent they could. Every person had a different take on it. They knew Mbasa Kilu could kick the ball high and long, but it was a circus trick. Why would this be valuable in U.S. Football? Some said it was just more of the craziness of U.S. Football. A few who had been quick with the *Not-Right-in-the-Head* gesture were quick to point out what they saw as the irony: What do you expect from a sport that would fly the likes of Mbasa Kilu across the ocean to play U.S. Football, when he couldn't even take the field against a bunch of Primary 3 students in his own country, playing real football? But these were only a few, and they were shut up in a hurry by those who wished to claim credit for discovering Mbasa Kilu's skill and genius.

The brothers at Maryville Regional, of course, were interested in Mbasa Kilu's progress — especially those from the U.S. who were fans of U.S. Football to begin with. During the regular season, reports came from CNN International, but only in the form of post-game reports, sometimes with no mention of Mbasa Kilu. Brother Brendan Hagan subscribed to the *Boston Globe,* and when the "MBoomer" item appeared noting his 81-yard kickoff the brothers were delighted. Sky Sports Unlimited also picked up the "MBoomer" item and featured video of the towering kick. From then on there was more in the news about Mbasa Kilu, including local stories about his growing years in the Maryville Region, his disability, his being the equipment manager of the Douglastown Leopards.

Then came the playoff game and Mbasa Kilu's injury. Early reports only noted the final score, the fact that it was won by a record-breaking field goal. Then reports described the subsequent kickoff, the game-saving tackle by Cook, the fourth-quarter standoff in a blinding snowstorm. Then video started to come in showing the towering field goal, followed by the kickoff in which Cook, Mbasa Kilu, and the Green Bay runner went down together. Finally pictures of Mbasa Kilu being taken off the field on a cart.

When word of this started to filter out, people who had no knowledge of football — U.S. or otherwise — became interested. Talk of the Revenge of the Great Spirit started to emerge again, and some shook their heads knowingly — *After all, what did you expect would be the outcome?*

As soon as they got word of the injury, Brother Jerome Jenkins thought to visit Grandmother Nona and reassure her about her grandson, though in truth the extent of his injuries was not yet known, only that he had been conscious when they took him off the field.

Later there was the call to Grandmother Nona from Gardner. And a couple of days later Mr. Raymond Perotta called Brother James Connelly. Perotta had not been at the game but had spoken with the team physician. "The doc says his feet definitely took the brunt of it," he said. "It was like putting a jig saw puzzle together. He'll walk okay when it heals, but they don't really know if he will kick again."

As soon as he was well enough Mbasa Kilu managed to call Grandmother Nona and Gardner, even spoke with Brother Jerome Jenkins. Ofi Leiya — seeing Grandmother Nona at the market or at church — always asked about Mbasa Kilu. With the various phone calls and what they could glean from his letters, people back home kept more or less up to date.

* * * * *

Meanwhile, Mbasa Kilu's rehabilitation proceeded without any setbacks. At first he distinguished his two feet by thinking of them as the painful foot and the excruciating foot. The painful foot on the right — broken ankle on that side, but less surgery on the foot — and the excruciating foot on the left — his kicking foot — "shattered," to quote Doctor O'Brien. At first he could not move either foot without pain.

But week after week, the pain started to dissipate. After a while, physical therapy helped. His feet, frozen at first, eventually could be moved: first a gentle flexing exercise, eventually a circular stretching and limbering. Mbasa Kilu had been used to his feet being a focus of every step he took. Sometime in the third month he started standing, with the therapist's help, by the side of the bed. First for a few seconds at a time, eventually minutes, leaning on a walker, venturing the first step behind the walker, then another.

At first his feet seemed cockeyed, as if they had been put on wrong. "They've been put on *right*," said the physical therapist. "Your chart says they were severely deformed before. Now they're straight. Now you are walking the way most people walk. You're just getting used to that."

The surgeon still stopped by a couple of times a week. He seemed proud of his work.

Next time Mbasa Kilu talked to Grandmother Nona he passed this on to her.

"I just hope they haven't done anything to hurt you," she said. She repeated what they had said at the Imperial Medical Center Annex in Brightwood Crossing. "You should have such surgery when you are younger," she said.

He assured her the doctors in Green Bay were very good, as well.

"I know," said Grandmother Nona. "Just be careful. Do what they tell you. And be sure to thank them." Then she added, "Whatever it is with your feet, Mbasa Kilu, I will always be proud of you. . . . And I love you."

* * * * *

Soon Mbasa Kilu started to mark his week by the number of hours to the next physical therapy session, or the next meal, the next broadcast of *Newshour*. Before long he knew every section of the Green Bay *Press Gazette* — by now taken with discussing the spring pitching prospects of the Milwaukee Brewers.

He did not often think about the fact that his kicking career had been suddenly and violently interrupted. Being a member of the New England Patriots had always seemed a bit outlandish to begin with. What made him think he belonged here, instead of on the practice pitch in Douglastown? Separated from his home and separated from Gardner and his teammates, he would feel a touch of loneliness. But then a physical therapist would appear to put him through his paces, bringing him back to the real world of the rehab wing — a world separate and distinct from both his football world and his Douglastown world.

* * * * *

Mbasa Kilu's conversations every few days with Grandmother Nona helped him overcome the loneliness. But in the rehab ward — especially before he could walk — he woke every day to the same four walls, eventually to the same tiled corridor. It was a special occasion when he was taken to a different therapy room.

A second blue envelope arrived from Ofi Leiya, with a letter. On the phone, Grandmother Nona told Mbasa about seeing Ofi Leiya the previous week. She had asked Ofi Leiya to explain the warranty card that came with the new TV. "I was so glad to hear from Grandmother Nona that you are getting better," Ofi Leiya wrote. "She is enjoying her new TV."

Then she talked about her life, which was taken up with Martin and her new job, working for Mr. Munkasy at the hardware store. Martin was doing well in pre-school. Mr. Munkasy had gotten a new computer for the store, and she had learned how to use it.

Ofi Leiya had looked up Wisconsin on the Internet, and had seen photos of snow. She asked him what snow was like.

Martin had colored another picture for him. This time it was a house with a tree in the side yard. Stick figures on the front porch represented Ofi Leiya and Martin. The front gate was standing open.

"We will be glad to see you when you get home," Ofi Leiya wrote. "Love, Ofi Leiya and Martin."

The letter and card from Ofi Leiya also helped with the loneliness.

* * * * *

Gardner called Mbasa Kilu every week. "Just to check in," he said. They wouldn't talk long. Just gossip. What's going on in therapy? How is the pain? Gardner was thinking about buying a restaurant in Natick. "Just a step above a diner," he said. Then he had to explain what a diner was. "Jeffcoat's, on Post Road, where you had the clam cakes," he said. "That's a diner." Sometimes Gardner had news of the team: Potter had his knee surgery; Worthington signed a three-year contract. The first five games on their schedule next year would be playoff teams from this year.

Once Mbasa Kilu asked if he had heard from Cook. "Number 34 Cook," Mbasa Kilu said.

"I know who you mean," said Gardner. "I think Cook has . . . What? Three years? Maybe three years before he's a free agent. I don't think he's going anywhere."

Saturday afternoon, about ten days after they had this conversation, Mbasa Kilu heard someone saying his name at the nurses' station. A minute later Cook's smiling face appeared in his doorway. Mbasa Kilu was still staying off his feet, but Cook came straight to his bedside and embraced him. "Boomer, Bro! You're looking great!" he said.

Another man was with Cook: an enormous man. Close-cropped blond hair. Shoulders and arms bulging his leather jacket. He ducked his head coming through the doorway, stood back timidly as Cook greeted Mbasa Kilu. "You know Andersen," said Cook.

Then Mbasa Kilu recognized him. Andersen, number 78, offensive left tackle. He could see Andersen's broad back lined up in front of him as he prepared for a punt. "We'll keep them away from you," Cook had told him early in the season. And Mbasa Kilu realized Andersen was one of the main reasons

Cook could make this promise. "Hi, Boomer," Andersen said, shaking hands. "How you feeling?"

Both Cook and Andersen had attended Southern Illinois together and played together there before coming to the Patriots. Andersen was drafted by the Patriots second and Cook fifth in their year. The night before their visit Cook had come from his home outside Chicago and stayed with Andersen. Then the two of them had driven together from Andersen's home in nearby Seymour, Wisconsin.

Cook played master of ceremonies for the visit, asking Mbasa Kilu all the details of his injury, his therapy, his prospects for getting back to the Patriots. "Don't worry," Cook told him. "You'll be back out there." Then he paused. "This time," he said, "I'll try not to fall on you." Mbasa Kilu reassured him there were no regrets. "That's what football is," he said. Then he repeated what he had heard a TV commentator say. "That's what happens," he said, "when a punter tries to make a tackle." Which drew a laugh from both Cook and Andersen.

Cook didn't miss an opportunity to comment whenever a nurse came near. "You want to watch out for this one," he would say to Mbasa Kilu, loud enough to be heard in the hall. "Let us know if any of these nurses give you a bad time."

After a while Andersen came out of his shell. He had questions about Mbasa Kilu's life before he came to the U.S. "Where do you hunt?" he asked. He was surprised to hear that Mbasa Kilu did not hunt, in fact, never had. He brightened up when Mbasa Kilu described taking perch and tilapia from the Great River and nearby lakes.

"Have you told him about the baby?" asked Cook. "Show him your pictures, Bro," said Cook. "Talk about big! He's gonna be bigger than his daddy." Andersen had a three-month old son, and plenty of photos on his iPhone. Andersen appeared to be about a foot and a half taller than his wife, a beautiful woman.

"His college sweetheart," interjected Cook. "Can you imagine anybody that good-looking wanting to marry this ugly hulk?" Andersen just smiled.

The last picture in the series showed Andersen and his wife and baby on the sofa together, his arm around his wife, her cradling the sleeping baby in her lap.

As they left, Mbasa Kilu heard Cook making one last crack to the nurses, Andersen meekly reassuring them.

* * * * *

Rarely a day went by when Mbasa Kilu didn't reread Ofi Leiya's letter and card. Still, he wasn't prepared for the questions he got from a new physical therapist, there to do ultra-sound treatments. His name was Phil, and after the usual where-are-you-from questions he got right to the point. "Do you have a girl friend back home?" he asked. Instead of just saying "No," Mbasa Kilu answered "Not exactly."

"Oh," said Phil, "so it's like that. Sounds like you got somebody on the hook."

Mbasa Kilu wasn't at all used to this kind of talk — especially where Ofi Leiya was involved — and he felt embarrassed. "Looks like you're blushing," said Phil. Mercifully, he backed off a little. "Hey, don't feel bad," he said. "We all go through that." Phil then proceeded to unravel a story of his own on-again, off-again girl friend, before stopping to explain the next step in the ultra-sound treatment.

Fortunately, in the hospital Mbasa Kilu's roommates were usually post-op patients, there for only a day or two before being discharged. So they had not pried about his letters and cards from home, though he tried to be unobtrusive when he reread the notes from Ofi Leiya.

Rehab was different. The second bed in his room was sometimes empty, but when he had a roommate it would be for a longer period of time — weeks instead of days. This meant that there were longer periods of conversation between him and his roommate, and often the subject of wives and girl friends and family came up.

Guys in general knew that he was a football player for the New England Patriots, and it was easy to get the conversation into that area — at least away from wives and girl friends. One of the things he learned in the football conversations was how little he knew about the team's offensive strategy apart from the punting and kicking he was involved in. And how much the ordinary fan knew — from days of watching football experts talk in detail about the subject on the regular sports shows. He himself got to watching these shows with his roommates. He also found himself developing his own opinions of the game, not as much from his experience with the Patriots as from watching TV.

One of the hardest questions his roommates asked was one Kevin Bolt had asked him earlier. "How do you kick it so high and long?" Or: "How do you kick it exactly where you want it?" The answer was, he just did. He had learned one thing from Gardner: not to tell anyone he learned to kick from Grandmother Nona, even though it was basically the truth. Instead he might answer the question by repeating some of the wisdom Kevin Bolt shared about punting. Or things Coach Murka had tried to tell him, before they both came to realize that he had his own unique style, and it was unlikely to be improved by conventional coaching advice.

* * * * *

Some of the female physical therapists were Green Bay football fans and talked football with him. In general, though, they were more interested in the family type questions, the wives and girl friends area. He developed a standard set of answers for them, as well. Was he married? No. That was easy. Did he have a girl friend? Not at the moment. And that would settle it. No one was bold enough to go beyond that.

Mbasa Kilu realized, though, that every time the subject came up he thought of Ofi Leiya, seated in a rocking chair in her small living room, still wearing the white luyaà of mourning. By now the mourning period would be over: what would she be wearing now? How would she answer the question, Does he have a girl friend?

How would *he* answer it? He knew how he felt about Ofi Leiya. But he also remembered the embarrassing conversation he had with her just before he decided not to go with the Archbishop to have surgery by the Big Doctor in Indoniva. He remembered that she said he would make a good husband, but he also remembered coming to the conclusion that she meant *a good husband to someone else — not to her.*

Often, after such a conversation during the day, he went to sleep with these questions on his mind.

* * * * *

The day Mbasa Kilu was finally permitted to take real steps was cause for celebration. It meant walking like he had never before in his life walked — straight, without the characteristic wobble. It was a heady feeling, to be sure, even though his first steps were tentative. Grandmother Nona's friend had said that he was a handsome young man from his knees up. No longer were his natural good looks overshadowed by deformed feet. His steps got stronger every day. By April Mbasa Kilu could walk the length of the Vince Lombardi Rehab Wing corridor. Out the window, before returning to his room, he would glimpse the first buds on the trees in the chilly Wisconsin Spring frost. Doctor Jim O'Brien was pleased with the healing of the surgery. "You'll still feel some pain," he told Mbasa Kilu. "But over time most of that will go away." The best news he brought Mbasa Kilu, though, was that he could go back to Boston. "But no kicking," he told him. "At least not until the doctors at Mass General say it is okay." For the time being Mbasa Kilu was content to walk — without worrying about kicking.

* * * * *

Mbasa Kilu made the trip to Boston with only a cane. Gardner had offered to come and fly back with him, but he managed fine by himself. Meeting him at the airport, Gardner couldn't believe the progress he had made.

"You look a hell of a lot better than the last time I saw you," Gardner said.

Gardner had lined up all his cards and balloons in the dining room, and Mbasa Kilu read each one. "I don't know why people kept calling here," said Gardner. "It was like they didn't have any phones in Green Bay."

The team doc met him at Mass General Hospital the next day, and went with him to be X-rayed and see the doctor who would plot his recovery. The first thing the doctor did was examine the surgical site and the X-rays, pronounce the healing excellent.

"I know you're anxious to get back," he told Mbasa Kilu, "but I would like for you to take it easy at first." There would be no kicking, he said, until the muscles had strengthened and completely adapted to "the new architecture." To accomplish that he would go to physical therapy sessions at Mass General three days a week, exercising at home the other days.

Day after day his balance grew better. Mbasa Kilu was actually able to walk normally — without the characteristic wobbling gait. Walk, yes; but he did not yet run. He had not somehow blossomed into an athlete, but rather he was just a normal person — in fact, a normal person learning to walk.

* * * * *

And he became a U.S. citizen. After scoring 100 percent on the test and breezing through the citizenship interview, Mbasa Kilu was sworn in with 32 others at the Federal Courthouse in Framingham on Veterans' Day — the first member of the FasTrack program to complete the requirements. The Immigration Service made sure there were reporters and photographers at the ceremony. Stories appeared in local papers the next day. One picture showed him giving an autograph to the smiling Federal Judge who performed the ceremony.

* * * * *

Mbasa Kilu's first attempt since the injury to kick came with the season half over. The Patriots were doing okay, for them. But they lingered in third place in the Eastern Division of the conference. Clearly they could use Mbasa Kilu's soaring kickoffs, which had boosted them into the playoffs the previous year. There was a chill in the late November air when Gardner drove him over to the practice facility. Coach Murka was there, and one of the trainers, and Scotty, the assistant equipment manager. Murka shook his hand, said it was good to have him back. "You look a heck of a lot better than in that hospital," he said. It was the first Mbasa Kilu had seen Scotty and the trainer since back in Green Bay, as well. "Hey, Boomer," said Scotty, smacking his hand. And — to Mbasa Kilu's surprise — there was Malcolm, his PT from Mass General, who took him through 15 minutes of warm-up exercises before Scotty brought out a bag of footballs. Murka and Gardner stayed in the background and let Malcolm handle the practice.

Mbasa Kilu's first attempts at a punt felt awkward. Holding the ball, dropping it, timing the kick — that part of it felt natural. But actually contacting the ball with his foot was a completely different experience, like hitting a ping pong ball with a straw. His foot no longer felt like it was one with the ball, as it had since he was a child kicking in the lane in front of his apartment. Instead the ball bounced off his foot erratically. He felt as if he was giving the same effort as before, getting the same leg snap, but the ball was more a foreign object and less a familiar texture against his foot.

His first few attempts barely reached twenty yards. He tried to contact the ball more solidly but still fell short of thirty yards. When Malcolm saw him increasing the effort he called it off, getting Mbasa Kilu to go through a series of cooling off exercises, finally icing his foot and ankle.

"Okay," said Murka, "Good start, Kilu. We'll try again tomorrow. Same time. Same station."

On the drive home Mbasa Kilu tried to explain to Gardner how it felt. "When I was a kid," he said, "the first time I ever did this, it felt like the most natural thing in the world."

"Today was different," he said, "like I had never before done this."

The next day the same group gathered on the practice field. With one addition, the special teams coach, who stood talking with Murka and Gardner on the sideline.

Once again Malcolm took him through the warm-ups before Scotty broke out the balls. Once again Mbasa Kilu tried, and once again his attempts were unspectacular. Twenty-five yards, thirty yards, once or twice a bit over thirty.

"Okay, Kilu," said Murka. "It's still early." He looked toward Malcolm. "Maybe tomorrow we could try some place kicks."

"It's okay by me," said Malcolm. "Whatever he feels up to. I just don't want to give him too much all at once."

"I would like to try," said Mbasa Kilu.

My father didn't repeat this to Mbasa Kilu, but he said Murka had been despondent on the sideline. Murka said to him and the special teams coach that it was like watching his 11-year old kid learning to punt. "What happened to the 70-yard punts we saw all last year?" he said.

"Actually, though," said Murka, "he looks a heck of a lot more like a football player." "Not all the wobbling," he explained.

Next day Gardner himself held the ball for the place kicks. Gardner suggested they start at extra point range, kicking from the 10-yard line.

When Mbasa Kilu's first three attempts failed, the group became strangely quiet. "This isn't even a chip shot," Murka whispered to the special teams coach. "It should be a gimme."

The problem was obvious: the ball wasn't getting off the ground. After three more misses Gardner stood up. "Need to take a break?" he asked Mbasa Kilu.

But Mbasa Kilu wanted to continue. "I'm not getting any elevation on the ball," he said.

"I don't know what I'm doing wrong," he told Gardner. "Before — I never even had to think about it." His foot felt okay, he said. It just wasn't working the same.

From the twenty-yard line, one or two kicks made it over the crossbar. But for the most part they skimmed along at low altitude where any defensive lineman would have knocked them down. Twenty-five yards and up was out of range.

The next day was the same, as well as the three times they tried the next week.

At first he would talk about it to Gardner on the way home and at dinner, trying to discover the key to getting back in the groove. Eventually he talked about it less. Finally: not at all. Gardner said it was obvious he had given up on the idea of his ever getting his remarkable ability back — as had Murka and Gardner and those who watched him.

When my father told of this, he was near tears. "Here was this man who held the record for the longest field goal in history," he said, "and he couldn't kick an extra point."

* * * * *

The Patriots kept Mbasa Kilu on injured reserve the rest of the season, which ensured that he got paid for the entire season. But the season ended in late December with the Patriots' record at eight wins and eight losses, missing the playoffs. Gardner convinced the general manager to get Mbasa Kilu's signature on a contract for the upcoming season — a move that would be important later. He would be listed as a scout and assistant vice president of foreign personnel. Four days later Gardner drove him to Logan Airport for the flight home.

Book III
Flight

Section 7 — Back Home

Mbasa Kilu slept most of the long overnight flight home, waking briefly a couple of times in the darkened plane. He was surprised to wake a third time and find the plane landing at the huge regional airport in the bright sunlight. There he transferred to a smaller plane for the last leg of the flight.

Among the people waiting at the Sherbourne City airport was a young lad carrying a sign saying "MBASA KILU." Another boy beside him carried a sign on which was lettered "WELCOME HOME BOOMER." Then, behind these two, Mbasa Kilu saw the face of Brother Jerome Jenkins, who stepped forward and embraced him.

"I was afraid we would be late for the plane," he said, "waiting for these two to get their signs ready." He introduced the boys as members of Youth Football at St. Peter Claver. They seemed awestruck to shake Mbasa Kilu's hand.

"I almost didn't recognize you," Brother Jerome Jenkins said. "Compared to how you used to walk, this is amazing."

Brother Jerome Jenkins confirmed that Mbasa Kilu was feeling okay, that his feet and ankles were virtually without pain. On the drive back to Douglastown Mbasa Kilu talked briefly about his hospital stay and medical care and therapy in Green Bay and Boston. He couldn't bring himself to talk about the loss of his ability to kick, and he didn't want to put a damper on the excitement of his return home, so he didn't bring up his failed attempts to kick for the Patriot coaching staff, and Brother Jerome didn't ask.

After they were on the road for a while, Brother Jerome Jenkins told about happenings since Mbasa Kilu had been gone.

There was rebel activity around Mount Elliott and some of the mining towns. So far, not very organized, but it was said the miners were with them if it ever came to a showdown.

"We haven't seen much of it around the Maryville region," he said. "Occasionally people are stopped and robbed on the highway. But so far they haven't bothered us brothers, or the White Franciscan Sisters," he said, patting the cross he wore around his neck. It was well known that the rebels stayed away from the Mission Compound almost with a sense of superstition — afraid that the priests and brothers and sisters possessed some magic power that could repel them.

Around the Mission Compound Miss Rose was still Mission Housekeeper. A new Mission Caretaker had been hired, and Brother Jerome Jenkins ticked off his résumé — Mark Ndiko, a Maryville Regional Vocational grad, a grandfather and widower from Simpson Village, who had retired from being a supervisor in the quarry. "He doesn't get along with Miss Rose," said Brother Jerome Jenkins.

He also mentioned Ofi Leiya's job in the village, helping Mr. Munkasy at the hardware store. Martin was thriving in day care. Brother Jerome Jenkins looked over at Mbasa Kilu from the driver's seat. "Whenever I go in the hardware store she asks about you," he said.

Mbasa Kilu lost his breath for an instant, then muttered something about how she had always been considerate of him.

"You should go see her when you have a chance," said Brother Jerome Jenkins.

Then Brother Jerome Jenkins grew serious. "Marvin Kindola came around the other day," he said. "He says he urgently needs to talk to you as soon as you get in."

As soon as he heard "urgently" he thought of Tedu Ngraeba's unresolved murder and his suspicions about Marvin Kindola's involvement. But with the two boys in the car, Mbasa Kilu did not bring that up.

"Just so you're not caught off guard," said Brother Jerome Jenkins, "I think Marvin is looking for money."

* * * * *

When they got back to Douglastown Brother Jerome Jenkins stopped first at Grandmother Nona's house. She ran from the house in tears to embrace Mbasa Kilu. "Oh! Mbasa Kilu! My baby!" she said. "I was *afraid* something would happen. I was *afraid* you would get hurt." She buried her face in his chest and wept aloud.

Mbasa Kilu just laughed, and hugged her tightly. "But look at me, Grandmother Nona," he said. "I'm fine."

Neighbors came out on the street when they heard the commotion of his arriving. The two youngsters from Youth Football jumped out of the car and screamed, as if they had just realized who he was, inciting the other children in the neighborhood to do the same. The lady next door brought flowers and strewed them on the front walk. When they formed a line of dancing and singing, Mbasa Kilu and Grandmother Nona joined them. "*Ayuna! Ayuna!*" the people called out in unison.

* * * * *

Brother Jerome Jenkins arranged with Grandmother Nona that he would house Mbasa Kilu until more permanent arrangements were made, in order not to disturb her boarder. Of course the new Mission Caretaker, Mark Ndiko, lived in Mbasa Kilu's old apartment at the end of the Annex Building, formerly known as Moru Hall. So Brother Jerome Jenkins had Mbasa Kilu put his things in an extra room in the brothers' house.

When Miss Rose, the Mission Housekeeper, saw him and saw the new way he walked, she made a cross on her forehead. "Praise God!" she said. "Your Grandmother Nona has been praying for this day." "I suppose he'll be staying for supper," she said to Brother Jerome Jenkins.

* * * * *

(Brother Jerome Jenkins, who supplied all the details of the homecoming up to this point, finally got him to visit Ofi Leiya after sending him on a specific errand to the hardware store. There Ofi Leiya greeted him and insisted he come by and visit her. "To see Martin," was how she put it.)

(Initially Mbasa Kilu would not admit to his shyness when I interviewed him. "I visited her," he insisted. "Nobody had to force me." Nevertheless, most of the information about that visit came from Ofi Leiya, or from what I was able to read between the lines.)

* * * * *

Ofi Leiya had arranged that he would visit later that same week. After greeting her and marveling about Martin: how he had grown, the progress he had made — evident in the day care projects which she had displayed around the house — he sat down opposite her in the front room.

"Your feet," she said. "I am sorry about the injury. But you look wonderful. It looks like the surgery was a complete success." Mbasa Kilu assured her it had been, that the pain was gone, that the healing seemed to have been perfect. "It looks as if I am out of a job playing U.S. football," he said, "but I'll find something." "Anyway," he said, "it is worth it."

As they talked, Mbasa Kilu's mind wandered back to lunches beside Ofi Leiya in the school cafeteria, back to other conversations with Ofi Leiya: about spelling words, about speaking from the heart. He thought about the encouragement she always gave him. He remembered his fantasy about last minute goals in football games, about television interviews. He blushed as he remembered the embarrassing time he asked if she would be interested in him if he had the surgery. He knew that some of the things they talked about in those other conversations had come true, and had made his life better. And he knew that some had not come true, but had been just an imaginary part of his life. And some of the things he had *not* talked about had not come true, but had been just a dream — like being married to Ofi Leiya.

Ofi Leiya, for her part, asked him about his experiences in the U.S., about living in Boston, about what he had to eat, about Mr. Raymond Perotta, about Mrs. Perotta — Helen — about where their children went to school. She said she was proud of him for going to America. Not because he had done well, not because he was successful at U.S. football, but because he had the courage to try. "I knew you would do it," she said.

Mbasa Kilu thanked her. "You always encouraged me," he said, "and I am grateful."

Eventually, when their talking grew more quiet, and Martin fell asleep on the couch beside his mother, Mbasa Kilu knew it was time to leave, and stood to say goodbye.

"Thank you for coming," said Ofi Leiya, and she stood on tiptoe and kissed him goodbye on the cheek.

Mbasa Kilu was startled by the kiss. He thought about it all the way home. He thought about it when he entered the brothers' house. He thought about it until he fell asleep.

* * * * *

My father said he could tell from the sound on the wires that Mbasa Kilu was calling him from Douglastown — at 7:30 in the morning. He just "wanted to talk." Actually, he wanted to talk about what had happened the previous evening: the kiss; what did it mean?

"What does it *mean*?" repeated my father incredulously. "What do you *think* it means?" He couldn't believe he had to explain this. "Mbasa Kilu, this woman is very fond of you. She is doing everything she can to let you know. Think of the notes she wrote you in the hospital. You've got to let her know you feel the same."

Mbasa Kilu was silent for a few seconds, then asked Gardner how everything was going.

"*I'm* doing okay," said Gardner, "but it looks like you've got your work cut out for you."

* * * * *

(When I talked to her, Ofi Leiya said Mbasa didn't say a word when she kissed him. He seemed to stop breathing. At first she was afraid he was going to faint. Then she was worried that he might have a girl friend in the U.S.)

(Mbasa Kilu also remembered the kiss. He was reluctant to talk about a lot of things, but he admitted he was scared to death when she kissed him. He said he didn't know what to think. Was she just being nice? Or did she really mean it? At any rate, he didn't know what he was expected to do. He didn't want to make a fool of himself. He also told about the call to Gardner; that Gardner had encouraged him to tell Ofi Leiya how he felt about her. That, said Mbasa Kilu, thinking back to Gardner's advice, that would have required some thought.)

* * * * *

The same week Mbasa Kilu made his way to Tedu Ngraeba's grave. By now grass had long since covered the small plot, but it did not cover Mbasa Kilu's memories of the funeral. He still saw the flower-covered coffin being lowered into the grave; Ofi Leiya, collapsed under the burden of her grief. A tombstone had been erected in the time he was gone. Already it showed a faint coating of green after the rainy season. Under Tedu's name and the years marking his brief life were carved three words: HUSBAND — FATHER — TEAMMATE.

In his mind Mbasa Kilu added a fourth word: FRIEND. He thought of Tedu asking him to be equipment manager of the football team, reaching out to him before football practice, pointing *Good Health!* to him after a winning goal.

Did Tedu somehow know about his visit to Ofi Leiya? Did he know about the kiss? What did Tedu think about it?

He wanted to ask Tedu directly, *What did you think? Husband — Father — Teammate. Friend. What did you think?* He could only think of Tedu's reaching out to him, Tedu's encouragement.

He found himself thinking about Tedu as husband, as father. He thought of how devoted Tedu was to Ofi Leiya, how proud he was of Martin, how he protected them both.

Protected them in the past. Husband and Father in the past. But Tedu had now passed through this life to the next world. He could no longer be a husband and father any more than he could score the winning goal for Douglastown.

Then Mbasa Kilu could think only of Ofi Leiya. "I could be Ofi Leiya's husband," he said to himself. "I could be Martin's father." And from that moment he knew that's what must be.

* * * * *

Later that week, when the sun woke him from a sound sleep, Mbasa Kilu realized he was still sleeping on Boston time. He could hear the voices of the brothers going about the day's business. When he looked out through the curtain, he could see the sun high in the sky, the day already warm. A lone figure stood in the courtyard. He wore a hat pulled down over his eyes, but Mbasa Kilu recognized Marvin Kindola.

Brother Jerome Jenkins greeted him when he went for coffee.

"Did you notice who is outside?" asked Mbasa Kilu.

"He was out there when we woke up," said Brother Jerome Jenkins. "We invited him to sit on the porch and have a cup of coffee," he said, "but he said he was okay. He wants to talk with you." He said it sounded like what he had told him in the car — money. "As Marvin put it, an investment opportunity." He added this with a tone of irony: the brothers who had taught Marvin Kindola in high school had grown used to his exaggerations.

When Mbasa Kilu appeared, Marvin Kindola came up to the porch and sat in one of the metal lawn chairs; Mbasa Kilu sat in the swing.

Marvin went to great lengths to describe this investment opportunity as something other than betting on the outcome of football matches. He described it as investing in football. "It's the national sport," he said. He went on to make it sound unpatriotic *not* to invest.

Mbasa Kilu listened patiently. It wasn't difficult to understand why Tedu Ngraeba had characterized Marvin as tiresome. Finally, when he sensed Marvin Kindola was nearing the end of his sales pitch, Mbasa Kilu broke in to say that at the moment he didn't have money he could invest. He was finally able to get rid of Marvin by agreeing to think it over.

"You'll be glad you did," said Marvin. He said he would get back to him in a couple of weeks.

* * * * *

The following evening Mbasa Kilu received another visitor. He introduced himself as Tyler Zachary. He was vaguely familiar, partly because he was wearing a New England Patriots baseball cap.

When Mbasa Kilu didn't respond to his name, Tyler Zachary let him know who he was. "I was here a few years ago," he said, "about the underground storage tanks."

Then Mbasa Kilu remembered the Oakland Raiders baseball hat. "The Contractor's Big Man," he said.

They greeted one another, and Tyler Zachary made sure Mbasa Kilu noticed his New England Patriots baseball hat. "After I saw you on TV," he said to Mbasa, "I changed teams."

Apparently that was true in more ways than one. Tyler Zachary had also changed jobs: he no longer worked for the

Contractor. He had become a Field Agent with The Syndicate. "I report directly to Dublin," he said.

Then he lowered his voice and grew serious. "Marvin Kindola came to see you," he said. Mbasa Kilu nodded.

Apparently the Syndicate had been watching Marvin, tracking his moves. "I would stay clear of him," said Tyler. "You know he bets. Now he's in big trouble — with the Gang."

He proceeded to unravel Marvin Kindola's scheme to Mbasa Kilu, who would later be able to put it together with what he learned from Ofi Leiya, who of course knew about Tedu Ngraeba's problems with Marvin Kindola.

It started back before Douglastown's championship seasons. Marvin Kindola's scheme was not that complicated.

In fact, in the early years there was no scheme: he simply bet against Douglastown. But when they started to turn into a power and threatened to take the championship trophy, he turned to Tedu Ngraeba. Marvin Kindola offered to cut him in — 50-50. He didn't want him to lose the games — just ease up.

"He would not have cooperated," said Mbasa Kilu.

"Of course you're right," said Tyler. "But evidently Marvin didn't know his cousin as well as you knew him. He should have known Tedu Ngraeba would not cooperate. All the more so because they were cousins: Tedu wanted to avoid any appearance of favoritism."

When Tedu refused, Marvin talked to one of the referees. He worked it out with him that he wouldn't bet win-lose; he would bet on corner kicks. He always bet on the underdog: if they got more corner kicks than the favorite, he won the bet, even if the favorite won the match — which they usually did. The referee agreed to help by giving more corner kicks to the opponents — or by *not* awarding them to the favorite. For example, by ruling that the favorite team had last touched the ball before it went over the end line. Marvin and the referee split 50-50.

It turned out to be a good bet. First of all, it didn't raise the suspicion that a loss by the favorite would have raised. Second, the referee worked a different pair of teams each week — so the match didn't have to involve Douglastown — or Tedu Ngraeba.

The rest of Marvin Kindola's story sounded like a bad idea which had gotten worse. Evidently he still felt safe after his unsuccessful overture to Tedu Ngraeba. After all, Tedu Ngraeba couldn't go to the police — who were occupied with their own schemes of corruption and bribery, and wouldn't want to hear about it. Surely Tedu Ngraeba would let it drop. Ofi Leiya later confirmed that this is what she had begged Tedu to do.

But, according to her, Tedu Ngraeba thought otherwise. He confronted Marvin Kindola. "I know what you are doing," he said, "and I want you to stop."

But Tedu didn't mention the police. Instead, he threatened to turn the matter over to The Syndicate — since they controlled the betting sites. If it got out that the games were being fixed — in any way — it would look like The Syndicate could not control the integrity of the games: people would not want to place bets on The Syndicate's web site.

Marvin Kindola surely knew he was done for if Tedu Ngraeba fingered him to The Syndicate. Obviously afraid to approach The Syndicate himself, he tried to discredit Tedu Ngraeba by reporting him to the police. First he tried the story of Tedu Ngraeba's failing to promote the campaign for Party contributions. That resulted in the harassing arrests of players.

Mbasa Kilu interrupted. "Everyone knows about the arrests," he said, "but how did you know Marvin was involved?"

Tyler hesitated. "We knew because . . . because we knew," he said. "The Syndicate was paying someone within the police. Plus we were listening to Marvin's cell phone. He loves to hear himself talk."

Tyler continued. "Even though they arrested a few players, the police seemed unwilling to touch Tedu Ngraeba," he said. "He still walked free. At any moment he could have turned over evidence to The Syndicate."

So apparently Marvin made up a story: he told the police Tedu Ngraeba had evidence of police confiscating betting money before it was turned in to The Syndicate.

For Marvin Kindola this had been a desperate move, an educated guess. However, the report evidently struck a nerve with someone in the police department. Everybody knew The Syndicate was already paying a regular fee to the police to allow the betting sites to operate. But that was between them.

If the police were taking more on the side — which according to Marvin Kindola is what they were doing — The Syndicate would be furious.

From there things got out of control. One of the Deputy Police Commanders sent out a car to intercept Tedu Ngraeba and Jeremy Ogangwu when they knew they were on the way to Brightwood Crossing.

The officers in the car insisted they came upon the accident just after it happened. That Tedu Ngraeba had been careless and had driven off the road. Or perhaps he had fallen asleep. Whatever the case, Tedu Ngraeba was now dead, and Jeremy Ogangwu was left without a memory of what had happened.

"So with Tedu out of the way," said Mbasa Kilu, "Marvin Kindola was off the hook, and The Syndicate had not been tipped off."

"For a while it worked, though by this time we were monitoring Kindola's bets. We were starting to put two and two together," said Tyler Zachary. "Kindola continued to bet on corner kicks, and the referee continued to cooperate. It was a good bet. For the most part, the favorite still won, so there was no suspicion. And occasionally Kindola lost the bet, which also deflected suspicion. He and the referee split 50-50, and everybody was happy, and none the wiser."

Tyler Zachary stopped for a breath before he continued. "Then one of the gangs found out what Marvin was doing. They claimed they represented the Rebels," he said, "but they were just a bunch of thugs. The Syndicate would not accept their bets. So they approached Marvin and said they wanted him to bet their money for them."

"It was the last thing Kindola wanted," he said, "they were talking twenty times the amount he was working with. Plus they didn't understand the idea of spreading it out so it wouldn't draw attention. But he had no choice: the Gang would expose his scheme — or probably worse — if he refused." He said this lasted a few weeks, and he won a good deal of money for the Gang.

Tyler Zachary said that up until this point what Marvin was doing was small potatoes. The Syndicate had pretty much figured him out but allowed him to continue to see if he would provide a link to anyone else. Now, with the Gang's money, it was a much bigger deal. Not only was a lot more money involved, the Gang was a formidable and ruthless opponent — even to The Syndicate.

The referee Marvin had recruited was William Wamp from Mount Everett. He noticed that once Marvin started betting the Gang's money the bets were driving up the odds on the other team. So one match, without warning, he shifted his calls to favor the other team — and had someone bet on that team for him. Needless to say, Marvin lost a bundle. Worse, he lost all the money the Gang had put up.

The gang leader — suspecting a double-cross by Marvin Kindola — confronted him. Fearing for his own life, Marvin Kindola gave up the referee. In reprisal, the gang murdered the referee, then turned to Marvin Kindola to make up the lost bet.

"The way he lives," said Mbasa Kilu, "I don't know what he could make it up with."

"We know how much he lost on that one match," said Tyler Zachary. "There's no chance he will be able to make it up — savings or no savings."

Mbasa Kilu assured him that he had no interest in betting with Marvin Kindola — or investing, as Marvin called it.

"I believe you," said Tyler Zachary, "but I knew it wouldn't hurt to let you know. It's hard to predict what the Gang will do next. They already have a checkpoint between here and Brightwood Crossing." He had been stopped at the checkpoint on the way to Douglastown, detained while the guards got permission via cell phone to let him through.

He spent a few more minutes recalling with Mbasa Kilu their first meeting, back when the issue was the underground storage tanks.

"By the way," he said, "we liked seeing your replays on Sky Sports. We were sorry to see you get injured, but your feet look great."

* * * * *

In a few days Marvin Kindola was back. He approached Mbasa Kilu in the compound. "So," he said, "have you decided you would like to make some real money?" He was his usual cocky self, showing no evidence that he felt under the guns of the Gang.

Mbasa Kilu made it clear he would not be "investing."

Marvin didn't stay around to chat. "Don't say you weren't given the chance," he said, before driving off.

* * * * *

And then Marvin Kindola was gone — just like that. He didn't say goodbye; he wasn't seen leaving; he didn't check out of his apartment. He just stopped being around.

It sounded as if the Gang may have passed sentence. For sure, Mbasa Kilu didn't want anyone to draw any conclusion about his being involved; or that he *knew* where Marvin Kindola could be found. So he kept his thought to himself, not even sharing it with the brothers.

Instead, in a few days Brother Jerome Jenkins came to him, holding the front section of the Sunday paper. He showed him a headline on the front page, below the fold: *Gang Hit Takes Labor Exec;* and under that: *Gambling Debt Suspected.* Marvin Kindola's body had been uncovered in the brush, fifty meters from the highway between Brightwood Crossing and Oil City. He had been shot twice in the back, then through his ear and out the other side — a gang trademark. The brothers made little or no comment when they heard the news. Mbasa Kilu sensed that none of them were surprised.

* * * * *

Two more visits to Ofi Leiya ended with an innocent goodbye kiss from her, after an evening of small talk, without Mbasa Kilu's getting up enough courage to say he loved her — much less that he wanted to be her husband, that he wanted her to be his wife. He treasured her kiss, but was paralyzed at the thought of trying to return it — afraid of making a fool of himself. He made up his mind that on the next visit he would speak up and tell her. Ofi Leiya had invited him for dinner the following weekend — the perfect opportunity. He would tell her what he had never been able to tell her. He would ask her the question he had always been afraid to ask.

What he didn't know was that the next visit would take place three days earlier, on a Wednesday afternoon. He was surprised when Ofi Leiya showed up at the compound. Mbasa Kilu was in his overalls, trying to make himself useful while a guest of the brothers: he had spent the day with Mark Ndiko, trying to help him make sense of Miss Rose's rules for rotating yams in their bins so they all would get air and none would spoil over the winter.

Ofi Leiya had gotten off early from the store and was waiting on the porch of the brothers' house when he returned from the storage barn. She smiled when Mbasa Kilu approached, but the look on her face told him she was concerned — even afraid.

Mbasa Kilu apologized for his appearance and sat down on the porch opposite her. Apparently a message was left on her cell phone overnight. She played the message for him. "We know what you know," said a voice he did not recognize. *"Where did Marvin Kindola have his money?"*

Mbasa Kilu's first tendency was to ask, *What money?* Marvin Kindola had lost heavily when the referee, William Wamp, had double-crossed him. Marvin Kindola would be broke, or nearly broke, unless he had saved an unusual amount — and his lifestyle was not that of a saver.

"What could this be about?" said Mbasa Kilu, half to himself.

"Maybe . . .," said Ofi Leiya, and hesitated.

"Maybe what?" said Mbasa Kilu.

Ofi Leiya took a deep breath. "A month or so ago, Marvin Kindola came to talk to me. He had started an account in the bank. For Martin's education, he said. He wanted to do something to try to make it up to Tedu Ngraeba."

At first Mbasa Kilu wanted to cry fraud: that Marvin Kindola would pretend to do anything to make it up to the man for whose death he was indirectly responsible.

Then it all came together for Mbasa. The Gang was no doubt keeping tabs on Marvin Kindola. They saw him go to the bank, then to see Ofi Leiya. They immediately made a connection, assumed they could find out from her where Marvin Kindola's money was and retrieve some or all of it. And once the Gang got set on such a course, they considered it a point of honor to take it to its conclusion. At the moment, someone in the Gang was convinced that Ofi Leiya was their key to riches, and for this she was in danger.

Mbasa Kilu's mind jumped ahead — to someone more vulnerable even than Ofi Leiya. "Where is Martin?" he asked. It was a day Martin would get off early from Day Care and spend the afternoon with her at the store. "He is at the store. Velma is keeping him until I get back," said Ofi Leiya, "Mr. Munkasy's wife. I'll pick him up on the way home."

"Better you not head home tonight," said Mbasa Kilu. He knew Mark Ndiko would be known at the hardware store, so he caught him before he changed out of his work clothes and asked if he could pick up Martin and bring him back to the compound. "Something has come up," he said. "He should be brought straight back here."

Everything needed attention at once. He went to Brother Jerome Jenkins' office and told him about the mysterious phone call Ofi Leiya had received, that he interpreted it as coming from the Gang. He believed Ofi Leiya was in danger. Brother Jerome Jenkins agreed Ofi Leiya should not stay at her home. Brother Jerome arranged for Ofi Leiya and Martin to stay with Miss Rose in her apartment in the compound until things were straightened out. Miss Rose agreed, reassuring them that she would keep the two of them safe. "It's my apartment," she said, "and it is nobody's business who I have staying there." Mbasa Kilu knew that she had not missed a word of the conversations of the last hour, and thus realized the importance — the danger — of the situation.

For now, at least, everyone agreed that keeping Ofi Leiya and Martin safe was the number one concern.

* * * * *

Martin was delighted with the change in venue. He was up early the next morning and Miss Rose had him at the table for breakfast — perched in his booster chair — by the time Mbasa Kilu came in for coffee.

"Mr. Ndiko said I could help feed the chickens . . . ," he said to Mbasa Kilu.

"*After* you finish your breakfast," Miss Rose said.

"That's right: first I eat my breakfast," he added.

Miss Rose gave Mbasa Kilu a look of understanding across the kitchen: she realized the danger to Ofi Leiya and Martin and would be on the alert.

Ofi Leiya entered the kitchen with a full laundry basket and Mbasa Kilu realized she had already been put to work by Miss Rose. But after she put the laundry basket down, she and

Miss Rose turned and faced Mbasa Kilu: he was being asked to call the next move.

Not knowing what to do next, the best he could do was reassure them. "It's going to be okay," he said. "For right now, let's just stay in the compound. Go about your business here. We'll work it out," he said. "I'll work it out." He tried not to sound as uncertain as he felt.

* * * * *

Okay, thought Mbasa Kilu. That will work for a while. But how long can they be kept safe in the compound? How long before the Gang overcomes its superstitious fear of the crosses the brothers wear and reaches out for Ofi Leiya? Or Martin?

Certainly in the U.S. they would be safe. He would gladly buy their ticket. But they couldn't just *go* to the U.S. There was the visa, the application, the wait, trips to Sherbourne City — and they hadn't even started the process.

He also thought of the checkpoint Tyler Zachary mentioned, which they would have to pass through to get to the airport.

Then he remembered his own departure for the U.S. Mr. Raymond Perotta had watched him kick one day; a day later invited him to come and try out with the Patriots. There was no trip to Sherbourne City, no wait. Mbasa Kilu couldn't remember signing an application, or receiving a visa. Mr. Raymond Perotta had arranged it all for him.

He also remembered one other thing: he was now a U.S. citizen.

Mr. Raymond Perotta must know how to do this. He could do it for Ofi Leiya and Martin just as he had done it for Mbasa Kilu.

As for the checkpoint, Mbasa Kilu would have to work something out without the help of Mr. Raymond Perotta.

* * * * *

When Mr. Raymond Perotta answered the phone it was evident that he was just waking up. Mbasa Kilu had to repeat the story before Perotta was completely aware of what was going on. When he realized the danger to Ofi Leiya and Martin he became alert.

"Is she staying in the compound?" he asked. It seemed to reassure him that she was, and he insisted this must continue.

"As far as bringing her over," he said, "either she has to have a professional job — doctor, lawyer, professor — or a husband." He thought for a moment. "I can't make her a doctor or a lawyer," he said, "but she could always get married."

Mbasa Kilu momentarily lost sight of the goal — to get Ofi Leiya and Martin out of danger — and was seized by jealousy that anyone would marry Ofi Leiya. Tedu Ngraeba: that was one thing. Tedu Ngraeba and Ofi Leiya were made for each other. But he couldn't stand the thought that she would marry anyone else. "I don't know," he said. "I don't think she would do it." He felt the blood rising to his face. "Plus," he said, "I don't think there is anyone else in the picture."

"Anyone *else*?" said Perotta. "What's wrong with *you*? Isn't she the one who kept tabs on you in the hospital?"

Perotta pointed out that as a U.S. citizen, Mbasa Kilu could bring a wife to the U.S. He had been such a visible public citizen, so celebrated in the press, that it would facilitate her entry to the U.S. He would not be suspected of importing wives like the dozen or so men arrested each year for attempting to capitalize on their citizenship by charging a fee to marry a woman and bring her to the U.S.

Mbasa Kilu heard little of the explanation. Instead he felt himself losing all the resolve he had built up for his next visit with Ofi Leiya. He had talked himself into asking her the big question, but not like this. Not with flight to the U.S. the goal. How would he know she wasn't accepting just to get safe passage for her and Martin? How would he know she really meant it? "I don't know if that would work," he said.

He thought of the first time he had contemplated this. The question he had mistakenly blurted out to Ofi Leiya. The rejection. The embarrassment. He experienced it all over again. "I don't know how she would answer," he said.

"So," said Mr. Raymond Perotta, "you'll have to ask her." He paused until Mbasa Kilu acknowledged. "Let me know," said Perotta. "We don't have much time."

* * * * *

When he explained the phone call to Brother Jerome Jenkins, he was told the same thing. "I can't answer that, Mbasa Kilu," said Brother Jerome. "You have to ask her."

"Maybe if we both explained it," said Mbasa Kilu.

(When I interviewed Brother Jerome, this was a conversation that stood out for him. "I recognized a bad case of stage fright," he told me. "Or lack of self confidence. You name it." Whatever it was, Brother Jerome agreed to accompany Mbasa Kilu to talk with Ofi Leiya.)

* * * * *

Brother Jerome Jenkins and Mbasa Kilu found Ofi Leiya alone in the kitchen with a pan of green beans, starting supper preparations. They sat down around the table in the dining room. Miss Rose and Martin were working in the garden and wouldn't bother them.

After a few seconds silence, Brother Jerome nodded at Mbasa Kilu, who finally spoke. "We have a question," he said.

Ofi Leiya was silent.

"Mr. Raymond Perotta," said Mbasa Kilu, "when he came on the phone . . . " He started to explain that it was early in the U.S., and Mr. Raymond Perotta was just waking up. Then he realized that wasn't relevant.

"I explained the cell phone calls," he said, "the danger. That you were being threatened. And Martin, of course." He took a deep breath. "Mr. Raymond Perotta thinks you would be safer in the U.S.," said Mbasa Kilu.

"And?" said Brother Jerome, prompting him for more.

"Mr. Raymond Perotta thinks you should be married, since I am a U.S. citizen," said Mbasa Kilu.

Seeing Ofi Leiya confused by what was being said, Brother Jerome stepped in and explained. How the wife of a U.S. citizen was given entry, along with a child. That if she and Mbasa Kilu were married, the marriage certificate would cover her and Martin for entering the U.S.

The marriage certificate: here she stopped him.

"Will the marriage certificate mean . . . Will it mean we are really married?" she asked.

This is what I was afraid of, thought Mbasa Kilu. *She won't do it.*

"And Martin?" she asked. "Will it mean Martin has a father?"

Here Brother Jerome Jenkins had to think carefully. Not only what was the reality, but how to explain it.

"Actually," he said. "The marriage certificate — the piece of paper — is to enable you to enter the U.S. Father Victor will take care of that part of it. In addition to Senator Peabody, Mr. Raymond Perotta knows a lawyer who will help on that end."

"And Martin?" she asked.

"Martin," said Brother Jerome Jenkins. "Martin is not a problem. You have his birth certificate. Or at least we can get a Baptismal certificate from the church files. He's your son: if you get in, he gets in."

"So the marriage certificate is just a piece of paper? There's no ceremony? We're not really married?" she asked.

"I didn't mean that," said Brother Jerome. "There can be a ceremony, if you wish." He paused. "If *both* of you wish."

"Then there should be a ceremony," she said. She stopped and turned to Mbasa Kilu. "Mbasa Kilu," she asked, "don't you think there should be a ceremony?"

Mbasa Kilu's overwhelming thought, at this point, was that Ofi Leiya was doing it for Martin, for his safety. She was willing to go through a wedding ceremony, whatever it took, to get out of a situation in which her life and Martin's life were in danger. He admitted to me later that the thought of being married to Ofi Leiya — being *really* married to her — had started to evaporate. Not that *he* didn't want it, but that the only concern now was to get her and Martin out of danger, and that wouldn't be the same.

But of course he too wanted to do whatever it took for them to be safe. So he consented to a ceremony. "I agree," he said. "There should be a ceremony."

By this time Miss Rose had returned to the kitchen, leaving Martin digging in the garden. She continued quietly preparing supper — attentive to what was being said. That was part of what Brother Jerome Jenkins called his "strategy" for Miss Rose: she was going to find out what was going on, so he didn't shut her out of conversations; better she be in a position to hear it first hand than to draw conclusions from tone and innuendo. Also, by not actually inviting her into the conversation, she couldn't feel free to treat the information she overheard as her own, to distribute at will.

And, it turned out, she sometimes had good suggestions. For the last several minutes of the conversation, Miss Rose stood quietly near the door to the dining room, holding an empty mixing bowl. Now she walked to the door.

"Miss Nona," she said.

"Yes, Grandmother Nona," said Mbasa Kilu, "she too should come to the U.S."

"And to the ceremony," said Miss Rose.

"I'll see that she is told," said Brother Jerome Jenkins. "Mark Ndiko can pick her up. And we need to contact Father Victor about the ceremony. The rest of it, we'll work it out."

* * * * *

Anticipating their return call, Mr. Raymond Perotta had already got the ball rolling on the U.S. end. In addition to calling Senator Peabody, he also contacted the president of the Patriots, who agreed to use the organization's influence with Immigration.

"Marriage is not their favorite way of allowing someone into the country," said Perotta, "but we can make a pretty good case that Mbasa Kilu is not a scam artist. You still want to see that the certificate is in order."

Mbasa Kilu spelled out to Mr. Perotta the full names of Ofi Leiya and Martin. Then he raised the issue of Grandmother Nona.

Mr. Perotta paused. "You didn't want to make this any easier for me, did you?" he said. "The grandmother . . . She would be like a nanny for the young boy?"

Mbasa Kilu didn't understand "nanny."

"A nursemaid," Mr. Perotta explained to Mbasa Kilu. "Like a full-time babysitter." When he saw Ofi Leiya nodding her head, Mbasa Kilu agreed.

Mr. Perotta mumbled something about a green card, then spoke out. "Hey," he said, "that's why we're paying these guys $500 an hour. Let them figure it out."

Then there was the matter of the checkpoint, which assured that no immigration documents would be delivered to the mission complex. They agreed that the documents would be expressed to the airline counter, to be picked up on the day of departure.

* * * * *

Mbasa Kilu realized that everything that could be done had been done. There was the difficulty of getting to the airport, which he was working on. And the documents. Getting them issued. Getting them expressed to the airline counter. All these things were pieces of a precarious bridge that had to be crossed.

He also realized the things that were lost. The dinner Ofi Leiya had invited him to that weekend: that was lost. The question he had finally resolved to ask Ofi Leiya at that dinner: that was lost. The simple answer he had hoped to get from Ofi Leiya: that was lost in the shadow of the impending danger, which seemed to override everything.

He didn't blame Ofi Leiya for thinking about Martin's safety. That's what being a mother meant. But the situation made it impossible to guess Ofi Leiya's true feelings for him. Yet in the face of the danger it was unseemly to raise the issue. Better to let it ride, to carry out the plan, the ceremony, or the charade, whatever it was. Better to get everybody in a safe place, then sort it out.

For the time being, that safe place would be the Mission Compound, but only until the reservations and documents were in order, ready for departure.

* * * * *

Wedding ceremonies at St. Peter Claver church took place on Saturday mornings at 10am. If there were two: 10am and 11:30am. However, the ceremony that particular week would take place on Wednesday morning, 45 minutes before the first light of sunrise touched the complex.

Guests arrived by the glimmer of the security light on the corner of the barn.

Grandmother Nona arrived — not with Mark Ndiko, after a change of plans the night before — but with Mr. Munkasy from the hardware store, in his delivery truck. Grandmother Nona wore the dress she would have worn to the market later that day. Mr. Munkasy wore his regular blue denim shirt, with a plastic pocket protector, and three colors of pens — red, green, and blue. Mark Ndiko was already inside — preparing the church for a service.

Miss Rose walked across the compound to the church from the brothers' house, holding the hand of a youngster who hadn't been permitted out of the house for the last 48 hours while arrangements were in progress. She wore a dark print dress — with pictures of six different tropical birds — and her church hat. The youngster, of course, was Martin, who wore what he usually wore — a T-shirt and short pants — though today he was not barefoot as usual, but wore sandals.

Brother James Connelly was next to cross the compound from the brothers' house to St. Peter Claver church. He was with Brother Mortimer Ygloso, the shop teacher, who was willing to put aside his disdain for U.S. football for the day, or at least for the duration of the ceremony, to honor a local boy and girl, even though the boy had played U.S. football.

Brother Jerome Jenkins followed next with Mbasa Kilu, who wore the same clothes he had worn the night before, when he had helped Mark Ndiko replace the latch on the gate.

At the same time they were crossing the compound, a car drove up the road and pulled up to the front of St. Peter Claver church. Father Victor Woluska got out and went inside, adjusting the hood on the back of his cassock so that it lay straight on his back.

Inside the church, Mark Ndiko had left the electricity turned off, but arranged several lighted candles marking the path up the aisle to the main altar. He stood at the back, waiting for the ceremony to begin. Meanwhile, the other participants had taken their places in the pews, except Mbasa Kilu and Brother Jerome Jenkins, who stood waiting in the front near the altar.

Miss Rose and the boy entered the pew with Grandmother Nona, and Martin's young voice could be heard for a brief moment as she embraced him. For a few seconds, everything was quiet.

Then, outside, a door could be heard opening, then closing — the door from Miss Rose's apartment. Ofi Leiya stepped out first onto the front path, stopping to let her eyes become accustomed to the security light. Sister Ann McDermott followed her out, pulling the door shut behind her.

Ofi Leiya was wearing a white blouse and knee-length blue skirt like the one she had worn the day before when she did the laundry for Miss Rose, like the one the sewing ladies wore when they operated the looms, with sandals on her feet. Over the blue skirt she wore a filmy, transparent skirt which reached to her ankles, which caught the reflection of the security light across the yard as she straightened it out with both hands.

Sister Ann McDermott stopped and looked at Ofi Leiya when she stepped beside her. Then opened the gate into the compound, stopping to notice the new latch and pointing it out to Ofi Leiya. Together they walked across the compound, paused briefly outside the door of the church, and stepped in.

By now Father Victor Woluska had walked to the front of church and stood at the foot of the altar, facing the pews. Brother Jerome Jenkins and Mbasa Kilu stood to his left. People in the pews stood and faced the back of church as Ofi Leiya emerged from the shadows. She started to step down the main aisle, between the rows of candles, by herself. Then stopped and motioned Sister Ann McDermott to walk beside her, and the two of them walked down the aisle together.

Now from Miss Rose's arms Martin's young voice could be heard again as he discovered his mother and pointed to her, causing the others to smile.

* * * * *

Anyone listening to the ceremony would not have known it had taken place 45 minutes before dawn, by the light of the few candles Mark Ndiko had arranged. Nor would they have known that people wore their everyday clothes, including Mr. Munkasy, who reached into the plastic pocket in his denim shirt and produced the blue pen with which the wedding certificate was signed — first by Father Victor Woluska, then by Sister Ann McDermott and Brother Jerome Jenkins as witnesses, and lastly by Mbasa Kilu and Ofi Leiya. The signing of the certificate took place in the back of church, on the cover of the baptismal font in which the baby Martin had been immersed only three and a half years before. After it was complete, the group separated, heading in different directions — some of them never to see one another again.

* * * * *

Those who attended the ceremony would not linger. Mr. Munkasy and Grandmother Nona were the first to leave, in the hardware truck. Miss Rose watched out the window of the brothers' house as the truck left the compound.

"Miss Nona is gone," she said, barely loud enough for those at the dining room table behind her to hear. She had prepared boiled *fufilla* for Ofi Leiya's and Mbasa Kilu's and Martin's breakfast, with a special smiling-face design of blueberries in Martin's bowl.

The last two weeks she had taken to calling Ofi Leiya *child* when they worked together about the household tasks. *Child, could you unload the washer?* Or *Child, would you refill the yam basket?* This morning she said *Child, I'll take care of that.* And *Child, just leave the dishes — this is your day.*

Halfway through breakfast, Mark Ndiko came down the back steps from the second floor into the kitchen from the room where Ofi Leiya and Martin had stayed, carrying the crate in which Miss Rose's new convection oven had been shipped. He passed through the kitchen and out to the brothers' garage, just as Brother Mortimer Ygloso walked across the compound to help him load it into the brothers' pickup truck. Martin was sitting at the side of the dining room table with his back to the kitchen and did not notice. Nor did anyone else take notice — except that Ofi Leiya at that moment pointed out a blueberry which Martin had missed, handing him a spoon to scoop it up.

While they were still eating Brother Jerome Jenkins appeared in the dining room door, paused for a moment, then sat at the empty end of the table. Sister Ann McDermott walked in just behind him, carrying a large handbag, stayed standing against the wall inside the dining room.

When they finished breakfast, Ofi Leiya brushed the crumbs off the front of Martin's shirt. "You'll go with Miss Rose," she told him. Then she took off the transparent overskirt which reached to her ankles and handed it to Sister Ann McDermott.

* * * * *

Mbasa Kilu realized that the time had come for them to leave. He couldn't help thinking that it was the first time he had sat down to breakfast with Ofi Leiya and Martin. Was it the first of many to come? Or the first and only? How did Ofi Leiya regard this new family group? No time to think about that. Just focus on getting them all safely on the plane.

* * * * *

Outside the sky was getting light. Ladies were gathering for the sewing session in front of the Mission Center Annex building, formerly known as Moru Hall, the fourth and largest building in the compound. A few had small children with them. Mark Ndiko was still busy inside the garage, and had not yet raised the great doors, so women and children waited outside the doors and in the center of the compound. As more arrived, their voices — and occasionally a child's voice — could be heard.

Sister Sheila McMurphy arrived for the sewing class, parking outside the fence around the brothers' house. Women walked across the compound to greet her. Some pointed to the garage, indicating that Mark Ndiko was busy and hadn't yet raised the great doors. Others seemed content to take advantage of the extra minutes of socialization. A few noticed that Ofi Leiya had come outside into the back yard of the brothers' house. They let themselves through the gate to talk with her. Like them, she was wearing a white blouse and knee-length blue skirt, which they all wore when they sewed. They joked that she should join them for the sewing session — even though they knew that Ofi Leiya had already received her certificate of training signed by Sister Sheila McMurphy and was now Mr. Munkasy's top clerk at the hardware store. Others made a fuss over Martin — whom some of them had not seen for a while — and compared the height of their own children with that of Martin.

None of the ladies arriving for the sewing session could have guessed what had gone on inside the church in the hour before dawn. And none of those who had been part of the ceremony would breathe a word about it.

Finally Mark Ndiko emerged from the garage and crossed the compound to raise the great doors of the Annex building. Women drifted to their places, the sound of their voices soon replaced by the whirring of the sewing machines and the dull roar of the electric fans moving the air through the building and out the great doors.

After he saw that the sewing session was underway, Mark Ndiko crossed back to the brothers' garage to prepare for his first errand of the day, which would be to take the parcel in the convection oven crate to Brightwood Crossing in the brothers' pickup truck and post it at the Federal Postal Center — which increased the probability that it would actually be delivered to the address given, though this was still no guarantee that it would not be stolen and sold later on in the black market.

Then he would carry the rest of his cargo — now covered with a tarp — to the recycling center. There it might be recycled, though it was more likely to be scavenged and resold — also on the black market.

The brothers' pickup truck was the first to emerge from the garage, but Mark Ndiko pulled to the side of the courtyard and waited. Close behind him Brother Mortimer Ygloso backed the brothers' black sedan out of the garage and drove out of the compound first. Seated in the back was a young woman in a white blouse and knee-length blue skirt, apparently the mother of the young child seated next to her. When they reached the main road they turned and proceeded on the road toward Brightwood Crossing. Mark Ndiko followed a few car lengths behind in the pickup truck.

* * * * *

Before this procession of two vehicles was even five kilometers down the road they encountered the checkpoint: a pickup truck with its emergency lights blinking, a man at the side of the road motioning them to stop. Though he held an AK-47 the man was not in the uniform of the police or the federal soldiers. Instead, he was dressed in the rag-tag manner of the Gang, who characterized themselves as a resistance group — though what they seemed to resist most was the idea that they should be deprived of their share in the graft and plunder enjoyed by members of the government. But this day they seemed to have a different mission. Wearing sunglasses, his AK-47 pointed skyward, the man motioned the sedan to the side of the road. Three others stood behind him, all in sunglasses and dressed partly in civilian clothes with some fragments of uniforms. Two held ancient combat rifles; the third, who seemed to be in charge, wore a sidearm and carried a cell phone in his palm. Clearly the sedan was the car they were looking for, especially when it became evident there were no passengers in the pickup truck. Impatiently one of the other men waved the pickup truck on and again directed Brother Mortimer Ygloso to pull the sedan off to the side. It was clear they were waiting for the brothers' black sedan because of the two people in back — the young woman in the white blouse and knee-length blue skirt and her little boy.

But when the leader approached the car and looked in the back, there was indeed a young woman in a white blouse and knee-length blue skirt — but no little boy: only a little girl with pigtails wound around the top of her head. When they checked ID cards, it was not the woman they were looking for but Louise Umbilla, from Douglastown, who produced an appointment card. She was taking her little girl to the regional clinic in Brightwood Crossing for eyeglasses. After also checking Brother Mortimer Ygloso's ID and having a brief conversation on the cell phone, the leader waved the car on. By now the pickup truck had disappeared over the next rise in the road.

* * * * *

These two vehicles were not the first to leave the Mission Compound that morning.

Forty-five minutes ahead of them, Mr. Munkasy continued in the hardware truck on the road to Sherbourne City. Beside him sat Grandmother Nona in her everyday clothes. The two had been quiet for most of the drive. Occasionally they commented about something outside — flocks of birds waking up and filling the trees with their noise; the first rays of the sunrise off to their right; the difference in the appearance of the ploughed fields as they approached the coast.

They too passed the checkpoint but were not even motioned to stop when it was evident that the truck carried nothing of value and the only passenger was an elderly woman. They did not talk about or even mention their destination, which was the great medical center in Sherbourne City — except for Mr. Munkasy to go over what Grandmother Nona would do there, what she would say. Grandmother Nona several times opened her purse and fingered an appointment card indicating her 1pm appointment in the diabetes clinic. In her mind she went over what she would do and say.

Meanwhile, the errand on which Mark Ndiko set out turned out to be longer than it first appeared. When he reached the roundabout outside Brightwood Crossing he did not take the branch toward the Federal Postal Center, where he could post his parcel, and from where it was just a minute's drive to the recycling center. Instead, he steered the brothers' pickup truck onto the next exit from the roundabout, leading to Sher-bourne City and the airport.

* * * * *

As the three vehicles continued their separate trips, it was not yet dawn in the U.S. Nevertheless Mr. Raymond Perotta had been on the phone for an hour after waking up his secretary and instructing her to contact the head of the Patriots' personnel office, ensuring that Mbasa Kilu was officially listed as an employee, that the contract he had signed before leaving was officially recorded. He would not be on the player roster, since his time on injured reserve had expired. But he would hold the position of scout and assistant vice-president of foreign personnel. It took some explaining to get across the idea that next week was not good enough to complete the appointment, that Mbasa Kilu would be on a flight arriving today, and it needed to be a done deed. He thought of arranging an appointment for Ofi Leiya as well, but given the difficulty explaining Mbasa Kilu's situation, he decided to leave well enough alone. And there was Mbasa Kilu's grandmother. *Let's get them into the country first,* he thought. *We'll make them legal later.* He had already smoothed the road for that by the packet of documents he had expressed to the airline counter for Mbasa Kilu.

His next call was to verify with Passport Control and Immigration at Logan Airport in Boston that the documents Mbasa Kilu and his wife had would get them through the arrival process.

When this was done, he went to the kitchen and joined his wife, Helen — also awake early — for morning coffee. He mentioned that it would be Ofi Leiya's first trip to the U.S. "I'll be able to go with you," she said. They agreed it would be good for her to be there for Ofi Leiya. "And the grandmother," she said. "Can you imagine?" she said. "All her life, she hasn't been away from home. Now this."

Mr. Raymond Perotta glanced at his watch and saw that it was just after 6am — eleven hours until they arrived. "But right now . . .," he said and trailed off. "Let's hope it's going okay right now."

* * * * *

Mr. Munkasy was the first to arrive at his destination, pulling up in front of the Sherbourne Memorial Medical Center. A steady swarm of people passed through the revolving doors, mostly going in, many wearing medical garb, some carrying stacks of books. Mr. Munkasy kept Grandmother Nona one last minute before letting her go. "Straight through these revolving doors," he said. "The queue is out the doors on the other side of the lobby." She nodded.

"And what do you say?" he said.

She repeated the instructions she had gone over with him on the drive from Douglastown.

"Good," he said. "Nona, safe trip. God go with you."

"Thank you," she said. "And thank you for the ride. I'll be fine."

* * * * *

Mark Ndiko was not completely familiar with driving in Sherbourne City, so he took advantage of the momentary pause entering the first roundabout outside the city to stop and read the signs. It was too long a pause in the judgment of the drivers behind him, who immediately sent up a din of anxious horn-blowing. Nevertheless he read systematically until he saw the sign showing the profile of an airliner, indicating the airport. He then eased the pickup truck into the roundabout and took that exit.

Immediately he noticed an increase in traffic, a wider road — followed half a mile later by a backup of traffic where a road crew had set up their markers and were now doing repair work. He satisfied himself that it was still early in the day and tried to retune the truck's radio to a station in the city.

* * * * *

Louise Umbilla watched from a nearby chair in the waiting room of the eye clinic as the technician tried one pair of frames after another on Ceci Umbilla. Louise had already told her daughter she could choose the frames herself; now she just hoped she would not settle on the pair with the orange stripes. Ceci finally selected a pair that was sky blue, and the technician proceeded to measure her for the right fit.

In the main lobby of the building Brother Mortimer Ygloso finished absorbing all the European football scores from the night before. He glanced at his watch, wondering if he had time for a second cup of coffee from the snack shop before the mother and child were ready to return.

Normally he didn't have the job of ferrying people back and forth to the clinic, but he realized this was a special case. He wondered if Mark Ndiko had yet completed his delivery.

* * * * *

Once inside the hospital's lobby Grandmother Nona hesitated for only a second before seeing another set of revolving doors straight ahead. She resisted the impulse to check and make sure she had money, instead tucked her purse tighter under her arm and walked to the other side of the lobby and out the double doors.

Outside, she saw exactly what Mr. Munkasy had described: three or four cabs discharging passengers along the curb to the right; to the left a queue of cabs waiting to be engaged. She walked directly to the first cab and got in the back seat, gave her destination, made no response as the driver curiously looked her over in her everyday dress.

As soon as the driver pulled forward *1,000 Tilotas* flashed up on the meter, and Grandmother Nona *then* opened her purse and looked at her money.

* * * * *

By this time Mark Ndiko had not yet completed his delivery, though he had navigated three of the four roundabouts on the outskirts of Sherbourne City and was still on the right track to his destination — and on time.

When he reached the fourth roundabout he glanced at the signs, then at the directions Brother Jerome Jenkins had given him. Straight across was *General Solomon Gambwizi Terminal,* but he chose the exit before that: *Post — Freight — Shipping.* He drove behind several larger trucks until they came to a guard shack, where a man in a brown coverall motioned the larger trucks toward a row of loading docks. Mark Ndiko stopped the pickup at the guard shack. At the same time he spotted the large folding door beyond the loading docks and motioned toward it.

"I have a delivery for Gabriel," he said.

The man glanced at the oven crate and tarp in the back of the pickup, flipped open a cell phone in his hand and pushed a number. "Tell Gabriel the guy is here," he said.

By the time Mark Ndiko had steered the pickup halfway across the lot, the folding door began to open. The pickup truck disappeared inside, and the door closed behind it.

* * * * *

Mbasa Kilu was relieved when the tarp finally came off the frame under which he sat. He himself did not mind riding in the back of the pickup. And fortunately Martin — after being awake early — slept most of the trip. But he was concerned about Ofi Leiya, and glad for her sake that the ride was completed, and without incident. If only that was the extent of his anxiety about Ofi Leiya!

First he had worried that she would reject the arrangements surrounding her going to the U.S. — namely the marriage ceremony, if that is what you could call it. But then she seemed to *want* the ceremony, to embrace it. Was this play-acting? A mother will do anything for the safety of her child, and if she had done this for Martin, he could understand it. But in the meantime, how was he supposed to act. Should he try to act as if they were indeed married? Whatever the answer, now was not the time to be thinking about it. Inside the giant warehouse there was a continuous hum of fork lifts moving palettes of goods up and down aisles of shelves. Just after the pickup stopped Mark Ndiko got out of the truck and lifted the tarp. A second later the man known as Gabriel embraced him. A man 15 years younger than Mark Ndiko, Gabriel carried a clipboard and seemed to have a supervisory function in the shipping warehouse. He ordered two of his men to remove the convection oven crate from the truck and lift the frame that had supported the tarp. He helped Ofi Leiya and Martin down out of the truck, and made a fuss over Martin. "What a big boy!" he said "Riding in Mr. Ndiko's truck. All that way!"

He also shook hands with Mbasa Kilu. "Sorry about your injury," he said. "But you can be proud of what you did in the U.S. I'm no expert about U.S. football, but you showed them a good Maryville man can compete with the best."

Mark Ndiko clapped Gabriel on the back. "Maryville Regional," he said to Mbasa Kilu, "just like you and me."

Gabriel showed the calluses on his hands. "He got me my first job — in the quarry," he said, indicating Mark Ndiko.

The oven crate was pried open, three suitcases removed. One Mbasa Kilu recognized as his own. Another was a tan case with brown stripes around the center which he recognized from Grandmother Nona's house. The third was powder blue, probably Ofi Leiya's, he thought. And the idea of her clothing and personal effects only reminded him of the anxiety he was trying to avoid.

"The shuttle will take you to the ticket counter," said Gabriel. "Your mother should be waiting for you there."

No need to explain it's my grandmother, thought Mbasa Kilu.

"It's all inside the terminal complex," said Gabriel. "There won't be any problem. Anyway, it pays to be careful."

* * * * *

Grandmother Nona was seated in the row closest to the ticket counter when the shuttle pulled up. When Martin saw her he ran to hug her.

She was anxious to describe the taxi ride to the airport. "He was a nice young man," she said, "and I gave him a tip: one hundred tilotas. And the *Ladies* is right over there," she said to Ofi Leiya, nodding in the direction of the rest rooms. "Has this child had anything to eat?" she asked. "I'll take him for a bun while you do what you have to do."

While the others went off in different directions, the shuttle driver took Mbasa Kilu to a vacant spot at the counter, where he was able to receive the packet of documents Mr. Raymond Perotta had expressed him. Everything appeared to be in order, and Mbasa Kilu sorted out what would be needed to check in when the others returned.

* * * * *

By the time they were ready to board the plane, Mbasa Kilu was feeling less and less certain about where he stood with Ofi Leiya. The trip to the U.S.? Sure, that had to be: she and Martin were in danger. This was their way out.

And yes, they had gone through the ceremony. But that too was part of the plan. The ceremony made the certificate valid, the certificate proved they were husband and wife. Not wanting to spoil the plan, he had agreed.

Mbasa Kilu was roused from his thoughts as the line started to move forward. He held Martin and the boarding passes — and the carry-on bag, which contained things Martin needed. Ofi Leiya walked beside Grandmother Nona, who held on to her purse.

First would be a short hop to get them out of the country. Then the long flight to the U.S.

* * * * *

The short hop was taken up with keeping Martin happy, fussing over his needs, real and imaginary. The four had to be separated when they transferred to the overseas flight at Rui Pol. That had to be the point at which Mbasa Kilu must decide to make it known that he did not expect Ofi Leiya to live up to her participation in the "wedding." After all, the ceremony was done to protect Ofi Leiya and Martin from the danger they were in. When they got to the U.S., that would be solved — so what better time for Mbasa Kilu to show how he felt about the deal? He would do so in how he arranged the seats: he and Grandmother Nona would sit apart from the others, leaving Ofi Leiya to take care of Martin — her usual role.

Except that he did not take Grandmother Nona into account.

"Martin and I will sit apart from you," she declared in the boarding line, taking the two boarding passes out of Mbasa Kilu's hand. "We'll be fine. And I can call you if we need you."

When Mbasa Kilu started to protest, Ofi Leiya took his arm. "They'll be okay," she said. And it was obvious Martin was looking forward to the undivided attention of Grandmother Nona.

So: there would be no "showing" feelings. Mbasa Kilu would have to tell Ofi Leiya straight out.

Ofi Leiya held onto him until they were in their seats. Even then she kept a hand on his arm, making him struggle to think of a way to say it. When they were in the air, it was Ofi Leiya who spoke first.

"Mbasa Kilu," she said. "You never asked me."

"Asked what?" he said.

"You never asked me to marry you," she said. "We were married this morning. We had the ceremony. But you still haven't asked me. Usually the man asks the woman."

"I th-thought," said Mbasa Kilu. He felt himself stuttering. "Once," he said. "Once I tried . . . I mean, it was a mistake. And I don't expect . . ."

She took his arm and squeezed. "Mbasa Kilu," she said. "Once? Once was different. Once I was Tedu Ngraeba's wife, and that was right. And I am Martin's mother, and that is right. And Tedu is his father, and that is right."

Ofi Leiya hesitated a second. "But now is now. And this morning we became husband and wife. And that is right." Ofi Leiya paused. "It is right if we both want it," she said. "I want it: I wanted it even before the danger came up. And you?"

Mbasa Kilu realized that as Ofi Leiya spoke her feelings, he felt as he felt when in school she first told him, *Look them in the eye, say what you have to say, speak from your heart.* So he looked Ofi Leiya in the eye, thought of what he had long wanted to say to her, and spoke from his heart.

"Your words make me happy," he said. "I too want it."

"Ofi Leiya," he said. "Will you be married to me?"

* * * * *

Epilogue

Parents and kids lingered after the game was complete. Mbasa Kilu greeted the other parents, patted the kids on the head. It pleased him to come with Martin to the games, to watch the grace with which Martin ran up and down the soccer field. He felt as if he were watching Tedu Ngraeba as a boy.

Martin called Mbasa Kilu *Papa*, even though he knew about Tedu Ngraeba, knew that Tedu was his biological father — though he could not remember him. And Mbasa Kilu would tell him stories about Tedu — as a young boy in school, as a superstar playing in the regional championship, as a good and honest man.

Sometimes Ofi Leiya came with him to the games, but today she had to take their daughter to the dentist. She would listen this evening as he described the game to her, as he described Martin.

Some of the parents, knowing his past life with the Patriots, called him Boomer. Most called him Bas, the nickname they had given him. A few called him Mbasa Kilu, struggling with the pronunciation and inflection.

For some reason one of the men asked Martin if he knew what a good kicker his papa was. "Sure," said Martin, "he taught me." Martin went on to explain that his papa could kick it the entire length of their back yard and still hit the net.

"I'm not talking back yard," said the man. "I mean *really good*." Which set up a hubbub among the kids, challenging Mbasa Kilu to show them how well he could kick. Kids jumped and shouted around him, and the men were loving it. Meanwhile Martin seemed confused by the claim the man had made.

"I'm surprised you haven't shown your son," said one of the fathers.

"Oh, Craig," said his wife, "maybe Bas isn't so anxious to give a special exhibition for *you*."

"Go ahead, Boomer, show them what you can do," said another of the fathers. Martin looked at his father with a question.

So Mbasa Kilu walked onto the field, over to the game ball, still lying in the grass. He lined up a couple of paces behind the ball, sighted the goal thirty meters away, stepped — one — two — and kicked. The ball whistled along at low altitude — a rifle shot — where only a perfectly positioned goalkeeper could have hoped to stop it. It hit solidly into the net.

Parents and kids erupted in applause. Several of the kids shouted "*Go-o-o-o-oal-l-l-l!*" mimicking the frantic scream of the enthusiast who called the soccer games on TV.

Mbasa Kilu turned to look at Martin's reaction. At first the boy seemed stunned, then remembered the gesture Mbasa Kilu had taught him. He pointed *Good Health!* to Mbasa Kilu, and Mbasa Kilu pointed *Good Health!* back to him.

★ ★ ★ ★ ★

That evening at home, after Mbasa Kilu described the game to Ofi Leiya and Christina, Martin had a question for him. "Papa," he asked, "did you play in the championship with my father?"

When Mbasa Kilu told him he had not, Martin wanted to know why.

"Well, Martin," said Mbasa Kilu, "that is a long story."

And *this* is that long story; and that is why this book is dedicated to Martin.

www.ingramcontent.com/pod-product-compliance
Lightning Source LLC
Chambersburg PA
CBHW070035260626
47159CB00005B/2050